COINCIDENTALLY IN VENICE

First published by Romaunce Books in 2024

Suite 2, Top Floor, 7 Dyer Street, Cirencester, Gloucestershire, GL7 2PF

A catalogue record for this book is available from the British Library

Coincidentally, in Venice
Paperback ISBN 978-1-7391857-8-7

Cover design and content by Ray Lipscombe
Printed and bound in Great Britain

Romaunce Books™ is a registered trademark

COÏNCIDENTALLY IN VENICE

Sometimes the right one is there all the time

Kate Zarrelli

Romaunce Books

For Juliet

(she knows why)

Prologue

The Venetian Lagoon
14th April 2022

Ashley thought she'd never forget her first sight of Venice. Because she wasn't in a James Bond film and was only on holiday thanks to a redundancy package, she wasn't surfing across the water of the lagoon on a speed boat but travelling on a *vaporetto* – in other words, she was on a bus. However, unlike the 159 to Streatham Hill, this one had never known a traffic jam. There was something romantic, Ash thought, even in the sturdy rumble of the boat's engine, the clunk as it nudged up against the landing stage where she and her best friend Juliet had embarked. There could be no sounds quite like those anywhere else in the world, she thought, and certainly no sights like this mirage of a city. Looking around the boat, Ash guessed that most of the passengers were holidaymakers like them, hardly able to believe that they were on the move again after so long. A few were clearly people returning home. They didn't look around the way the visitors did, nor scramble to get to the open seats in prow or stern. As the boat bounced confidently along she and Juliet gazed with open-mouthed wonder at the city rising out of the water, a cluster of bell-towers, bucket-shaped chimney pots, faded and crumbling façades and strangely eastern-looking pointed windows.

'We made it at last, Ash!' said Juliet.

'We did. End of a nightmare.'

'Start of a new life. And tomorrow we'll start looking for him. The webcam man.'

'And his dog. I wouldn't recognise him without his dog.'

Chapter One

London

14th April 2020

Ashley clicked through the webcam links for Venice. Each was more surreal than the last. There was St Mark's Square as it could never have been seen in its entire pre-Covid existence - empty. Pennants flapped idly in the breeze, advertising an exhibition at the Museo Correr that she'd read had been three years in the planning, but which no-one would get to see. The historic cafés, Florian's and Quadri's were shuttered. Not that Ashley had ever thought she would go to either place (she'd looked at the menus, and their prices, on-line). However she *had* been looking forward to drinking her morning cappuccino standing at a bar near the station, aware that it might cost her double if she sat down and had the waiter come to her, perhaps treble if she took a table out on the street to people watch.

It looked as though there was nobody in Venice now, but she knew that the dwindling number of people who always lived in the city must still be there, looking out of the windows of their apartments, listening to the silence. Some of the webcams showed barges laden with fruit and vegetables moving along narrow canals, unimpeded by the gondolas they showed on all the tourism sites, bearing tourists who looked as though they were dreaming about being in a Casanova biopic. Ash thought of the staff at the hospital at Zanipolo with its intricately carved Renaissance façade – and shivered at the thought of the nightmare they were experiencing now. She had done her homework and read history and guidebooks about Venice so she knew that over the centuries the city had suffered waves of bubonic plague. Covid too felt like a medieval threat; the only way to stop it seemed to be to avoid other humans, including the ones you loved the most. She thought of the chambermaids and waiters who in normal times flooded in on the train from polluted mainland Mestre every morning to service the raised eyebrows and clicked fingers of the tourists, now having to stay at home with fractious children who couldn't concentrate on schoolwork when all they could see of their friends were fidgety little Zoom images, occasionally enlivened by the appearance on-screen of a family pet. A lot of those children would have been born in that hospital on the lagoon but wouldn't have been able to afford to live there: Air BnB, she'd read, had been the final nail in the coffin for a lot of Venetians trying to find an affordable home, turning their city into a vast expensive holiday let.

But imagine having 'Venice' on your birth certificate. I've got the Chelmsford and Essex Hospital, and that'll have been turned into luxury flats by now.

Ash had seen the photographs on-line of shimmering jellyfish in the still waters of the Grand Canal, ducks waddling along the Riva degli Schiavoni in place of the endless tide of tourists, selfie-sticks and waving pennants or umbrellas held up by their tour guides. *I'm pleased for them, anyway,* she thought.

She sighed and picked up her phone. Thumbs moving fast, she sent a WhatsApp to Juliet.

Gorging on Venice webcams, hun. What about you?

The reply was immediate.

Gorging on Venice webcams, of course. Hey, we'll get there.

'I wish we knew that,' muttered Ashley, though there was no-one in the flat to hear her. She hadn't seen a real-live human being for three days, though the fridge was looking a bit sparse – pretty much like the supermarket.

It would just be great to know when, she typed back. *Even if it's three years from now. Just something I could mark on a calendar and start ticking off the days.*

Her Mum had urged her to be philosophical when they'd spoken yesterday. 'Venice hasn't sunk yet, Ash. It'll be waiting for you, and you'll appreciate it all the more when you do get there. Bit like me and the shops in the Harvey Centre.'

Mum, bless her, sort of missed the point, thought Ashley.

Easier to talk like that when you were fifty-something and you'd done stuff. Three years between, let's say, fifty-two and fifty-five wasn't a big chunk out of life, was it? Three years between twenty-six and twenty-nine, for a holiday dreamed of for at least eighteen months in advance, was an eternity. The best years.

Ten to eight. Ash switched on the work computer that sat alongside her larger personal one and slipped on her headphones. She'd leave St Mark's Square up alongside her customer accounts screen – or Piazza San Marco as she practised saying when she was alone. Given that Covid meant she was alone most of the time she thought she sounded quite impressive by now. And she could always count Venetian pigeons when the lack of anything else in sight got boring. *Oh, what's this?* There was movement in the corner of the webcam image. Two policemen strolled into the empty square, their hands clasped behind their backs. They stopped in the middle of that vast space. What were they talking about? Ash saw movement under one of the arcades. A man was pushing a rubbish cart but furtively, as if he didn't want to be seen. Ash thought: *probably nobody ever notices him, except to step around him. And now 576 people are on-line watching him.*

I like the webcam at the Rialto Bridge, wrote Juliet. *There's a seagull perched on a post who looks like he's in charge.*

These days he is, typed Ash. *Oh look, there's a vaporetto.*

Only two people on board apart from the driver.

Essential workers.

Do you ever wish you were an essential worker?

There was a pause, then **Juliet is typing** flickered.

Don't know if I'd have the courage, seeing what they're dealing with now, but what we're doing feels pretty pointless. After this I'll definitely want a change.

I know. This job feels like deck chairs on the Titanic. Might be forced out anyway, wrote Ash.

I've my fingers crossed behind my back, Ash. As long as there's a package. I've been practising my dismayed face in the mirror, so's they can't know I'm going 'yaas!' inside.

Oh! Meeting reminder. Are you in trackie bottoms too?

Yup! But my shirt's ironed. Just don't stand up.

Ashley peered at herself in the Zoom image before pressing the 'join meeting' button. *Jogging bottoms they can't see, but look at that hair!* It was light brown, though Ashley really wanted to be blond, curly when she really wanted to be sleek. But continuing to tong it smooth when it had grown as far as her shoulders just made it look limp. Ash sighed. The only comfort was that everyone else was looking a bit shaggy. She took a deep breath and pressed the button, populating the screen with rows of heads. Only her boss Rupert Brant looked groomed. Ash thought Brant's glamorous wife probably had a hairdresser trapped with the couple in their townhouse in Notting Hill or wherever it was they lived. The poor man – for some reason Ash was convinced Wanda Brant would have a male hairdresser – had most likely got stuck there when lockdown came and didn't dare risking being stopped by the police trying to get home. *You've got an overactive imagination,* she told herself.

Juliet of course looked fab. She'd always been flamboyant, with that mass of nearly black wavy hair. She'd resorted to piling it up in a lovely messy bun. Ash thought that if Juliet wasn't her friend she'd probably hate her.

Ash composed her face into serious-work-impression as Rupert Brant launched into his usual pep talk, in which battening down the hatches and digging into the trenches and strapping up for a rough ride all featured. She didn't know how the man had been so successful in Marketing, as the images he was conjuring up for his minions (as she and Juliet referred to themselves) meant she didn't know if she was supposed to be on a boat in a storm, an extra in Blackadder Goes Forth or holding onto the metal bar across her lap on the Sky Drop in that theme park in Southend that had dominated school holidays. Weren't you supposed to get across a coherent message to your customers – for Rupert Brant was always reminding people that their colleagues were customers too? Only she'd never come across a customer she'd want to have a drink with and talk to about her Ed troubles. That was strictly Juliet's department. Ash tried to concentrate on what Rupert was saying, judging the right moment to give the understanding nod signal, or do that interested tilt of the head manoeuvre that would make him think that (a) she was actually listening and (b) that she thought his tired old clichés were really original and inventive.

To be reluctantly fair, though, she thought the firm - Gulliver and Brant to give its full title though nobody she knew had ever met Gulliver - had been pretty bullish about the future. And flexible. They'd switched fast to on-line working, only how much work was there? Marketing and PR contracts weren't exactly thick on the ground. The car advert Ash and Juliet had been working on had been shelved. What was the point, when hardly anybody could get out and drive their cars anyway, and all the dealerships were closed? Extra training had been organized, even if Ash knew as well as anyone that there was a limit to how much of that would be put on before the pretence that this was just preparation for the great surge back evaporated. This morning's session was on sales techniques, though neither she nor Juliet, nor most of the people there, were in sales. Rupert Brant evaporated, having introduced the trainer for the morning's session. Ash could see the man was wearing a fleece. Behind him was the clean-lined foyer of a modern office, all granite and chrome, with a blurry figure frozen in the moment of walking downstairs. Alvin was going to teach them 'fun techniques' in a tone of voice suggesting he was really auditioning for Blue Peter even if he looked like a personal trainer who knew he was getting too old for the job. Ash wondered if Alvin was his real name. Perhaps his

Mum had been an Alvin Stardust fan – he looked about the right age for it.

As the morning wore on, they learned about funnelling, asking a series of questions until the customer felt they had chosen what you had to sell because its features and benefits made it blindingly obvious, not because you'd backed them into a corner. Ash didn't like the idea of selling but was pleased that other people liked doing it as at least it kept her in a job, beavering away behind the scenes, getting the details right in every package. But she kept telling herself it was useful to know about things like selling even if you didn't do them. It helped you decide what jobs you *didn't* want next and was as good a way as any of passing work time when everybody knew there were no new projects in the pipeline.

Inevitably, Ash's attention wandered off from the speaker's powerpoint to the tiles of little wobbling heads. Yes, she liked her colleagues, missed them and their Friday lunchtimes in the pub, and would have rather seen them in the flesh, instead of against the backdrops of the spaces they'd really only used for sleeping when life was normal. But there were some surprises. Big, stolid Joe in Accounts for instance. He had a mural behind him - a classical landscape, though when he'd been asked along with everyone else to say where he was dialling in from, he'd said Croydon, not a place Ash would have associated with Arcadian artwork.

Had he painted it? Others had family photos though she'd never remembered them mentioning these people or what they might mean in their lives; Ash gave herself a black mark for never asking. Some had cottoned on to downloaded images, which meant that Ned from IT and Nirmala from Customer Service were both apparently sitting in the same ancient library, until they fidgeted and Ash caught a glimpse of a shimmering halo of a magnolia wall or a kitchen cabinet.

The wall behind Ash was blank. *A bit like my life.*

Two days later Ash discovered the webcam of Campo Santa Maria Formosa. Only five people were watching, compared to several hundred looking at nothing moving except pigeons in St Mark's Square. The image was slightly distorted, so the bell tower of the church at the far end of the square was slightly curved. The camera was fixed quite high up, doubtless on the façade of the hotel which advertised itself in the strapline. The strutting pigeons outnumbered the watchers: there were no people to be seen.

She pulled herself back into what she was supposed to be doing – another company training course – minimising the image of the deserted square on her own pc. Alvin was back, his voice edged by an enthusiasm that was almost manic. He was telling his audience that they were about to go into break-out groups. Ash suppressed a sigh.

Later, when everyone was on a virtual coffee break, Ash wrote 'popping to the loo' in the chat box and deactivated her video image. On the other computer she googled the name of the hotel and feasted her eyes on polished floors, frescoed ceilings, framed paintings of the Grand Canal and Murano glass chandeliers – not to mention vast beds under muslin-draped canopies. Not a bit like the two-star hotel near the station she and Juliet had booked. *Hey, now nobody is staying in any hotels, expensive or dirt cheap. Covid, the great leveller.*

Ash caught herself up then. She'd seen the telly reports of Italian army trucks driving from hospitals to morgues, shots of coffins piled three or four deep in a church. The country was in the eye of the storm. How long before it was as bad as that in London?

How's your Venice stalking going? wrote Juliet that evening.

There was a man with a dog out today in that piazza I told you about. I've found it on the map.

They've got to have a pee too. The dog, that is. But I wonder how that works. Not much in the way of waste ground in Venice.

I didn't see. They went around the corner. Perhaps the pooch knows to pee in the canal.

Pooch? I thought you liked dogs.

I do. Especially this kind. He doesn't look like a breed though. He's white and fluffy but bigger than a handbag dog. There's a bit of terrier there from the way he moves around.

What about the man?

Can't make out much. I think he's youngish, just from the way he walks. But everybody on webcam looks like Lowry matchstick men. He's not giving away as much as the dog is. You can see he's over the moon at getting outside. Sniffing at everything. But obedient. There's no sound but he keeps coming back to the man.

Well, you know what they say about dog people looking like their pets. What's Italian for terrier?

I've just looked up terrier. It's the same word.

I bet there's a sexy Italian way of saying it, though.

Sexy? It must be at least three months since I've had a sexy thought and now I'm supposed to have one about terriers?

Steady on. That'll change.

That's what this holiday was supposed to be about.

Ash, I'm sorry. It will get better.

No, I'm sorry for whinging. We're alive, aren't we?

And so's the man with the dog. Perhaps he got it from the Rescue people.

Perhaps he could rescue me too.

That's my girl!

The man was there at the same time the following day. This time he was out for longer. Ash saw him leaning back against the marble well-head in the middle of the square. *This is where I find out if he smokes,* she thought. But his hands stayed in his pockets. Finally, he fished out a phone. Ash thought she could see him scrolling, then he straightened up, holding the phone in both hands. The dog was sniffing around doorways, looking hopefully up at a shuttered bar.

It's hard to see but I think he's texting.

Ash tried again to tell how old the man was. It was also difficult to say how tall he was, as there weren't other people to compare him against, but when she'd seen him moving out of sight with the dog, she'd thought his legs looked lean and his shoulders quite square. *Is that dark hair, or some kind of woolly hat?*

Eventually, he turned round looking for the dog. He must have whistled or called then, as she saw the terrier come trotting back to him from the door of the church. The only sound on the video, she'd discovered, was classical music, something vaguely Venetian with a harpsichord, that really didn't match what she thought was the mood of the man in the puffer jacket on a dank, misty day in March. And of course she couldn't listen to music anyway. She was supposed to be listening to the post-pandemic strategic plan.

Then a word cut through from the other screen. Twenty tiled heads were suddenly alert. 'Restructuring,' said the General Manager. 'The need to be lean and responsive when we finally emerge from the cellars, blinking in the light of our new world.'

Channelling his inner Bladerunner, wrote Juliet in the chat box. Ash's heart turned over before she realised that the message was only addressed to her. Ash didn't dare reply. *It'd be just my luck to copy everyone in and his dog.* She glanced back at the other screen. The man and the dog were gone.

Chapter Two

Streatham

20th April 2020

Ash was tipping pasta shells into a pan of boiling water when WhatsApp pinged on her phone. Her heart sank when she saw the message from Ed. 'I should have blocked him, like Jules said,' she thought.

You could have been here now, with me. Not stuck in that dump on your own. But then you always were obstinate.

'Damn!' muttered Ash. 'Why did I have to read it straightaway?' The phone vibrated for a second before it rang in earnest. Incoming WhatsApp videocall. Ash hesitated over Accept or Decline. 'Hell, he's seen the two blue ticks. He knows I'm here.' Ash tapped 'Decline.'

You bitch. Who do you think you are?

Heart pounding, Ash dialled Juliet on video-call as another message flashed up at the top of the screen. *The minute this lockdown diktat finishes, I'm coming round.*

'Block him!' she told herself. But then she thought, 'If I

do that I'll not get any warning he's coming here. And it's bound to make him madder. I could just delete his messages.'

Juliet's face appeared on screen, or more accurately, a blurry outline of her head, which looked enormous, with the light behind her like a halo.

'Hang on,' said Juliet. The phone stopped moving; Juliet had propped it somewhere. 'Just washed my hair,' she said, vigorously towelling her head. 'Hey – what's wrong?'

'Ed.'

The towelling stopped.

'You too making up?' Jules sounded wary.

'No. No. He's messaging me. He's well pissed off. Says he's coming round when lockdown lifts.'

'I've never asked you this, Ash. Probably I should have. But did he ever hit you?'

'No. He didn't need to.'

'No man should need to hit a woman – or anyone really. Don't answer him. But don't delete the messages either.'

'Should I read them?'

Ash saw Jules take a deep breath. She could see her friend thinking.

'Here's what I would do. Read them once a week, let's say on a Monday morning, about the time you'd usually have coffee.'

'I have coffee just about all of the time now.'

'I know. Everything is pretty weird. I mean the time we'd usually go for coffee in the office – 10.30 or whenever it was. Remember what the HR lady said about keeping to a routine when everyone is working from home?'

'We might never be back in that office.'

'Quiet, you. Let's deal with the Ed issue first. He sees when you read them, right? He's less likely to phone you back the minute he sees the blue ticks if it's a workday. Those IT people he works for have probably rigged his flat up so's they can tell if he so much as takes his eyes away from his work screen. You've an alibi for not talking to him during office hours. You'll also be sending the message – by not sending a message, I mean – that contact with him isn't that important or you'd be looking for him over the weekend when you'd have no excuse for not picking up. I wouldn't delete the messages if I were you. Just in case you ever need them as evidence. I know the plods are about as much use as a chocolate teapot about stalking, but you never know.'

'Thanks, Jules. You're a mate. I only didn't answer because I really, really don't want to speak to him. But time was, I would have done. Every time he clicked his fingers.'

'What changed, Ash?'

'It was when he phoned when lockdown was announced and said I'd better come round with a bag. Otherwise we wouldn't see each other for who knew how long, not until "mass house arrest" as he called it came to an end. I just thought – that's my chance. I didn't even know I was going to say what I said when I did, about suggesting we should give ourselves a break. I didn't really admit to myself that I was even thinking it. It was just when he said that otherwise we wouldn't meet for weeks and weeks that I felt this big surge of hope. I didn't want to see him. I wanted to know what life would be like without Ed. It's better, Jules.' Ash reached for a tissue.

'Why are you crying, then?'

'Relief. Sheer bloody relief. Just a minute —' Ash blew her nose loudly.

'That's my girl. Proud of you, mate.'

'Omigod. Forgot the pasta. It'll be sludge.'

Ash didn't know if the man was a creature of habit but the dog, being a dog, certainly was. She got quite used to seeing the two of them come out and walk around the square. She copied and pasted into Google Translate articles she read on Italian news sites; restrictions in Italy were pretty fierce. A Youtube video of Italian mayors going out and berating people for playing ping pong and looking out to sea had caught fire on the internet; one irate mayor, masked and wearing rubber-gloves as he filmed himself, had told them to get home and onto their Playstations instead. Necessary comfort breaks for dogs were allowed, though one of the mayors had gone online asking how it was that suddenly all the mutts in his town were incontinent. One person per household could go to the supermarket to get basic necessities. Ash hadn't yet seen the man with shopping.

That morning she signed up for Duolingo Italian. It

was one thing to assume that everyone working in a city so dependent on tourism would speak English in order to sell you something, but what if you wanted to talk to someone properly – *you know, someone who lives there?* She texted Juliet to tell her she thought Dog Man had a wife because she couldn't figure out how he was feeding himself. There was no answer.

Juliet wasn't on Zoom the next day to hear the General Manager *not* talk about the restructuring. Joe in accounts was insistent for news, asking what the process was going to look like, but all he got in response was a breezy 'you'll all of you be the first to know of any changes. And you'll be involved directly. We value you. You are the people who make this company what it is.'

Ash thought Rupert Brant was reading from a prepared script. Nobody else backed up Joe's lonely protest. Ash didn't know what to say either but wanted to show some solidarity with a man she'd barely interacted with when they'd both been in the same office. So she addressed him directly in the chat box.

Well said, Joe. Thank you for raising the issue. She pressed send even if she thought her message a bit lame. Joe's face was as impassive as usual. But just as the meeting was coming to an end, his reply popped up: *Thank you, Ashley. That means a lot.*

Ash couldn't help feeling though that Joe needed to get out more, but then didn't everybody these days?

Half an hour later her WhatsApp pinged.

My Gran's in hospital. We can't go and see her.

Oh I'm so sorry, Juliet. Thinking of you – I know how special she is. Here for you whenever you need me.

The second tick to say her message had been read took a day and a half to appear. And then Juliet phoned, hysterical with grief.

Chapter Three

London

July 2020

Three months later the announcement was made. It wasn't
a restructuring. It was curtains. Ash didn't feel the euphoria
she'd expected. She didn't even feel anxiety. Rupert Brant
was suitably solemn, going on about how every effort had
been made to keep things going, to maintain people's jobs.
The company had been bought over, and the buyer didn't
want the baggage of employees who 'might not share their
vision.' The chat box comments were illuminating. Ash
hadn't thought of her colleagues as being capable of so
much rage, so much emotion. Nirmala was openly crying.
Joe in accounts, whom Ash guessed knew what was coming,
had abandoned his usual shirt and tie in favour of a faded
Grateful Dead t-shirt; *out of uniform he looks almost good-
looking.* He was unshaven and he hadn't made his usual
attempt to tame his lockdown hair. She'd only known him as
placid and a bit stiff. Yet here he was typing furiously *you've*

seen yourself right, of course. You flogged the company to the highest bidder. Where next, boss? Bermuda?

'I know how you must be feeling,' intoned Brant.

No you don't. How dare you say you know how anyone else feels? God, are you?

Even on Zoom Ash could see the delighted outrage of the tiled heads. Nirmala was blowing her nose and attempting a smile. Rupert Brant was droning on but he'd lost control of the meeting. In the chat box what had been a greasy, stagnant canal of polite assent had transformed into a river in spate. Joe dammed the flow for a moment by writing '*I've got my deal already, guys. Careful what you say until you've got yours.*'

As the meeting broke up, the General Manager promising each employee a 'personal Zoom face to face with myself and HR about your package,' Ashley watched each of the tiles disappear one by one, like lights going out. *I'm going to miss them – they deserved better. The job? Not so much. And I'll still have Venice, one day.*

'The meeting has been terminated by the organiser' flashed up on her screen. Ash switched off the work PC, wondering idly if she might get to keep it. Who'd be bothered to come and collect hardware from all those people? She turned to the other computer and went to the webcam.

Dog Man was in a ferocious argument with someone. Ash felt the tension crackle off the screen, even without sound. That someone was a woman.

He's alone again, typed Ashley two days later. *Apart from the dog, that is.*

On Wednesday...
It's raining today.
I can see that!
In Venice, I mean! He's got a brolly.
Who? The dog?

Friday
I know where he lives. It's right on that square. I've seen him get a key out and go in though I can't see the building properly. It's right at the edge of the screen. Other times he walks straight towards the camera as if he was going into the hotel, though he wouldn't be, would he? You wouldn't need a hotel if you lived a few feet away.

If I didn't know you better I'd say that was creepy.

Tuesday.
The woman is back.

Hang on, I'll get on... They don't seem to be arguing today.
They're not holding hands though.
She could be his sister.
Nobody argues with a sister the way they were.
They look sort of used to each other. Not in the first flush of love, then. Perhaps they're married and separated and they're working out the divorce.
Oh.

22

Thursday.

I wonder if they realise they're being watched. You know, the way you turn round because you can sense someone staring at you?

We could go and stand under one of the CCTV cameras in the High Street to see how it felt.

Are you allowed to stand around in the High Street these days? Anyway, we'd already know we were being watched. That's what the cameras are there for. How would you know if you didn't know, is the question?

That sounds too philosophical for me. I think we have to go to Venice and ask the man if he knew we were there.

Don't you dare!

Our secret.

Yet Ashley felt her face heat up. How *would* she react if she ever met that man? Would she ever be able to tell him he'd been spied upon for months? Jules was right, it *was* creepy.

'I wanted to thank you personally for all your dedicated hard work over the last four years, Ainslie,' said the Rupert Brant.

In her tile, with its generic image of a foyer that looked nothing like the company they'd all worked in, the HR Manager raised her eyebrows.

'It's Ashley, and it's three years,' said Ash. *Who on earth would be called Ainslie? A left-back for Raith Rovers?*

The manager uttered a practised little laugh. 'Forgive me, I've had so many of these calls to do. People start to blur after a bit, you know.'

The HR Manager closed her eyes. Ash saw Rupert Brant lean to the side and take a sip of something from a glass. It was ruby red, but she was pretty sure it wasn't a fruit tea, even if it was only 9.30 in the morning.

'Perhaps I'll leave you with Cora, then. She'll explain all the details.'

'Bye,' said Ashley and looked expectantly at Cora. Rupert Brant disappeared without a sound. Cora was wearing a pussy-bow blouse and black jacket. Ashley was pretty sure she'd never seen her in anything other than a dark suit.

'Have you just the one jacket, Cora?'

Cora gaped. 'Oh! Well, for work I've six suits. One of them is usually at the cleaners. It has quite upset my routine, I can tell you, what with lockdown and everything.'

An image of Joe in Accounts in his Grateful Dead t-shirt and that Arcadian landscape behind him flashed through Ashley's mind. She felt a surge of sympathy for Cora. Joe quite possibly had A Life, whilst poor Cora got up every day and put on a suit – Ash was sure she wore tights and heels even though nobody saw them on Zoom – because doing so *was* her life.

'You've seen the package and I'm sure you'll agree it's a generous one.'

It was, but Ashley wasn't going to say so. She was now

on a growing WhatsApp group and Joe had posted there that the terms were good because the company was skating round the edge of legal requirements – a bribe in other words.

'I'll take it and shut up,' said Ashley.

'Well, if I just explain the terms…'

Ashley let Cora run on. The woman was like those people in the bank contact centre, she thought, who were obliged to read their spiel and you were obliged to listen to it before you'd the chance to ask your relatively simple question.

'It's OK,' she said, when Cora came to an abrupt end, as though someone had pulled a plug out. 'I've signed. But what are *you* going to do now?'

To Ashley's horror, the woman started to cry. It was like watching someone take a paper bag and crumple it.

'I don't know… I've never been out of work and it terrifies me. I really liked this job and I thought you were all so *interesting*. I hate it when things change – it puts me all out of sorts. I have to take acid reflux tablets. I know I can do a decent interview and I think I'm competent. Ask me anything about employment case law …'

For a moment Ashley genuinely wished she could.

'Only I get anxiety attacks when I meet new people – apart from when I'm interviewing them, of course. Because I'm in charge then. Employers think I'm loyal, but it's only fear really. I stay because it's scary to go anywhere else.'

Cora paused to blow her nose. Ashley wasn't surprised

to see her use a sharply ironed handkerchief.

'There's going to be a leaving do, of course.'

'What, eat out to help out?'

'Well, no. It'll be online. But the company will be sending some money for you to buy food and drink to eat at home.'

'Hey Jules.'

'A video call, no less. What's up?'

'Ed's found out about Gullible and Burnt,' said Ashley. 'He sent flowers this morning.'

'Ugh! Like a wreath?'

'No. Red roses.'

'I didn't know they counted as emergency items.'

'Perhaps they should, or they might if they'd come from anyone but Ed. Omigod, that's a mean thing to say, isn't it?'

'Not really. He wasn't exactly polite to you last time you heard from him. Have you answered him?'

'No. There was a text too, the minute he knew the roses had been delivered. I broke the rule and didn't wait until Monday – because of the flowers – and because Monday's like any other day now and he knows it.'

'So, what's he saying?'

'Same old. Move in with him, let him look after me. We were meant to be together. Think of the redundancy as a sign. *He's* had a promotion. Something to do with his "quick response to the techy challenges of lockdown."'

'What my granddad called having a good war, then.'

Chapter Four

'I'm enjoying this more than I thought I would, Jules.'

'Me too. Nice of Cora to organise it. *Cin cin!*

Ashley loved the sound of flutes of prosecco clinking, coupled with the view across the Heath at the end of a glorious day. It hadn't started out that way. The lowering clouds over Streatham when Ash had signed on to her temp contract that morning had reflected her mood and the thought of a reunion of old colleagues on damp grass that evening to hear about how they'd made a better job of the post Gulliver and Brant world hadn't filled her with enthusiasm. She was there only because Juliet had talked her into it, and because it would have been churlish not to have said hello to Nirmala and poor crying Cora. But quite a few people, it turned out, were in the same boat as herself, bravely calling themselves 'portfolio workers' who enjoyed their 'new found freedom,' though Ash recognised the muffled panic in their eyes because it's what she saw in the bathroom mirror every morning. She told herself off for her selfish relief that nobody was boasting about some rip-roaring career breakthrough. Everybody was taking what they could get to keep paying the rent; some, including Nirmala, had gone back to live with parents – in her case, in Neasden.

Ash put a hand on Juliet's arm. She was never quite sure if you were allowed to touch people, but she'd hugged Cora. The woman had looked like she needed it.

'Am I imagining things, or is that Wanda Brant over there by that tree? With those two web architects or whatever they call themselves?'

'Hang on, let me turn on the Botox monitor. Beep beep beep. Yup, that's her,' said Jules. 'Bit of a cheek. The bloody woman looks more expensive than ever, too. Hope her Manolos get stuck in the turf. No sign of our esteemed leader by the looks of things.'

'He'll have stayed behind in Bermuda. She probably got a broken nail and had to fly back to get it fixed. As long as she doesn't come and talk to us.'

'Who would have told her about this do? She's not on the WhatsApp group,' said Jules.

'Nor likely to be after Nirmala renamed it Gullible Survivors.'

'Better than Once Burnt Twice Shy. Talking of shy – isn't that Joe Mannion? I thought he was more one of those in the kitchen at parties types. Mind you, he looks a bit different.'

'He's coming over here,' said Ash. *Jules is right. He does look different. Longer hair, linen shirt and a lot less clumsy looking. Or maybe it's because I'm not used to men after being deprived of their company for so long.*

'Hello Juliet, hello Ashley,' said Joe.

'Hello Joe,' said Ash, wondering what else she could say. It wasn't as if she knew the man very well. She'd heard more out of him on Zoom in the closing weeks of Gulliver and Brant than she had in all the time they'd worked on the same open-plan floor.

'Not got a drink, Joe?' said Juliet, coming to the rescue. Or was she?

'I, oh... '

'Stay there. I'll go and get you one. Prozec do you?'

'Pardon?'

'Sorry, me being silly. Prosecco of course.'

'Oh, yeah. Thanks.'

Nope, still clumsy, thought Ash as Jules made her escape. *What's she want to leave me with Joe for?*

'How are you?' she said, conventionally.

'I'm good, actually. How about you?'

'Good, yeah. I'm on temp contracts. Figuring out where I'd like to work next.'

'Ted not with you?' said Joe, looking around.

'Ted? Oh, you mean Ed? I didn't know you knew him.'

'Um, well, I don't really. I just remember he was with you

at the last Christmas party.'

'2019 you mean. That feels like ancient history now. And so is Ed.'

'Oh, I'm sorry.'

Ash wondered if it was just a trick of the light, or was that a mottling of Joe's neck?

'*I'm* not.'

Joe smiled. *Never seen him do that,* thought Ash. *He should smile more often.*

'Well, I won't be sorry either, then,' he said.

There was a short, awkward silence. *Where's Jules? Has she gone to press the grapes?*

'I've a lot to tell you, Ashley,' he said eventually. 'I know it's not been easy for everyone here, but it turned out to be a real stroke of luck for me that G and B folded when it did. That and a couple of other things.'

'Really?' *He sounds pretty excited for an accountant.*

'I've taken a completely different direction.'

'Oh? Ernst & Young? PWC?' she asked politely.

Joe frowned. 'No. They're *accountancy* firms. I'm about to—'

'*Joe!*'

Ash turned in the direction of the squealing voice. *What on earth can she want?*

'Joe!' said Wanda Brant again, coming up and grabbing Joe's elbow. 'I need you over here.'

'I was just—'

The immaculately French-manicured fingers dug in as Joe threw a pleading look at Ash.

'What are you waiting for?' pouted Wanda, tugging him away.

Ash was watching the pair walk off when Juliet came back with three sparkling glasses.

'Oh! What's all that about?'

'Search me,' said Ash. 'But he looks like he's being led to the gallows. Belinda Botox never even looked at me.'

'Well, that's torn it.'

'Torn what, Jules?'

'Oh nothing. Which one of us is going to drink his prosecco? I thought he looked pretty good, didn't you?'

'I hadn't really thought about it,' said Ash.

'You know, a bit like that fellow in Poldark.'

'Aidan Turner?'

'Yeah. Wonder what he looks like with his shirt off?'

'I don't,' said Ash, thinking about Ed's ripped and waxed torso and hoping that Webcam Man wasn't another gym bunny.

'Where would we have been without Netflix, eh?' said Juliet, looking in the direction Joe and Wanda had gone.

Chapter Five

26th March 2022

Hello Jules. You're going to be mad at me.

We're still going to Venice, aren't we?

Three weeks and counting down. Try to stop me. No, it's to do with Ed.

Right, we're not doing this by text. I'm phoning you. Pick up, even if you're on the jakes.

'He messaged saying he wanted to meet me, that's all.'

'All? I hope you said a public place.'

'Starbucks on Streatham Hill. I never thought the safety training was going to apply to my own relationship.'

'*Ex*-relationship. Nobody ever does. Well, don't drink too much coffee with him because you'll be meeting me in Batch & Co straight afterwards.'

'Oh Jules.' Ash felt herself tearing up.

'So what does he want?'

'He thought as the Covid scam – his words, not mine,

was coming to an end and we could go back to being free human beings, we should enter the next stage of our lives as friends.'

'Hmm. Was he into conspiracy theories before Covid?'

'Not really. But then none of that was really put to the test. He was a bit vaccine-sceptic, right enough, but he got a full dose of the David Icke with Covid. All about how his body was a temple and he wouldn't inject it with poison. He'd had a screaming row with his Mum and Dad for what he called child abuse.'

'*What?*'

'He meant the vaccinations he'd had as a baby. I really liked his parents and I'm sorry I'll never see them again, but there was no reasoning with him. And you've seen how vain he could be—'

'That's more like it!'

'What?'

'Time was, you'd never have called him vain. You'd've just said he was taking care of himself.'

'I didn't like it much – all his working out. It was a bit obsessive.'

'Never liked a man with tits, myself.'

'Horrible, weren't they?'

'Ash, are you sure about going to meet him? Are you sure you don't want me to disguise myself with a stick-on moustache and that horrible old cap Dad wears on the allotment? I could sit two tables away and create a diversion by muttering to myself in an eastern-European accent to let you escape.'

'But we were going to get married!'

Ed was pale, his lips pinched. Ash thought she'd never seen him so emotional. She hadn't thought he did emotional. Just angry when he didn't get his way.

'Were we?' she said, bewildered.

'I'd only been waiting for my promotion to tell you.'

Tell me? What about asking me?

'I did well out of Covid restructuring.'

Ash looked for signs of commiseration for the fact that she'd been restructured out of Gulliver and Brant. *Nothing.*

'I was going to arrange a romantic holiday to do it in.'

'Where were we going to go?' she said faintly.

'We still could. I thought Venice. On a gondola.'

Ash closed her eyes. *We really don't communicate, do we? Did I not tell him that's where Juliet and me were going?* She wondered if she was going to think of Ed every time she saw a gondola. Then she pulled herself together. *Does it matter if I do?*

'Why throw it all away, Ash? After all we've been through. Just when things were going so right for me,' she heard him say.

'Oh, you know—'

'I don't.'

Ash's eyes widened. From the tone of his voice he

sounded as though he was conducting a performance review with a back-sliding minion.

'Covid, if you must know,' she said more sharply than she meant to. 'All that time alone to think. To consider what I missed. What I didn't miss. What was important and what wasn't.'

'God, you're hard!'

'I'm just trying to tell you what I feel.'

'Sounds like you were sorting through your wardrobe. Like they tell you to in those women's magazines. Sending stuff to the charity shop you haven't worn for a year. Or in your case, sending it *back* to the charity shop.'

The sneer was unmistakeable and Ash couldn't help rising to it.

'So you read those magazines?'

'I used to. While I was waiting for you to get ready. Well, let me just tell you something. You *were* important to me. I *did* miss you. We've been together a long time, Ash.'

'On and off.'

'Yeah, so we had our rocks in the road. But we got over them, around them. Proved ourselves. We knew what we'd have been getting into. You can't expect a relationship that long and stable to still be exciting, can you?'

Can't I? 'I just couldn't imagine us together in the future. But I am really fond of you, Ed.'

'*Fond?* I'm *fond* of my teddy bear.'

'I never knew you had one.'

'I don't, actually. Do I look like a man who'd have a teddy bear? But there's quite a lot you didn't know about me. I had plans, Ash, but you've pissed on them. I'm going places, you know. Our kids would have gone to private school.'

'Kids? Private school?' Ash gaped at him.

'Yeah. No comp for them. Or we could have moved out to Kent – some really nice properties out there – I'm a Kentish man, remember? They've still got grammar schools.'

Ash found her voice at last. 'You've got it all worked out. You probably even know the commute times.'

'You wouldn't have had to work once we had the kids.'

'But I like working.'

'No you don't. You were in a rut with Gulliver and Brant – said so yourself.'

'I… um. I only meant I didn't like *that* job.'

'Bloody hard to please, aren't you?' Ed scraped his chair back and pulled on his coat.

'You've not finished your coffee,' was all Ash could think of to say.

Ash's mouth watered just looking at her sourdough toastie.

'Seeing him hasn't ruined your appetite, then?' said Juliet.

Ash nudged her iron-framed chair closer to the table.

'No. It was OK, honestly. Well, not really.'

Jules looked beyond her friend to the long low window.

'Didn't follow you here then?'

'Nope. Flounced off even though I told him I was really fond of him.'

'Are you?'

'No, only regretful – sorry it had to take a worldwide health emergency for me to realise we really weren't good for each other. Ed just hates to lose, is the problem. I thought it was better to tell him a little fib about how I'd always be fond of him rather than a big fat greasy porkie like I loved him but we had to part.'

'Did he say the L word?'

'No. Though he did say he'd been intending to propose on a gondola.'

Spluttering, Jules put down her oat flat white. 'Cliché or what? Oops, sorry. I mean, look at me,' she said. 'I'm not exactly a success when it comes to men, am I?'

'I just thought you were doing market research,' said Ash.

Juliet laughed. 'That's a generous way to put it. Pity there's not a loyalty card for people like me. I could earn reward points, get somebody for free. I'm hardly qualified to comment on a long-term relationship, am I? But he wasn't good for you and I've always thought you should have more fun. I don't mean with lots of guys – I just mean someone a bit more – I don't know, eccentric or something. You're interested in stuff. He's only interested in access points and WANs – not that they're not useful things in their own way,

I'm sure. I've just never been able to imagine you with him, ten years from now.'

'I just can't imagine myself with him ten minutes from now. I've been mean too, treating him like a port in a storm, only in this Covid storm, I realised my boat wants to try for the high seas, not the safe harbour. And a bit of that old guff about better to have a boyfriend problem than a no-boyfriend problem. But it was creepy, Juliet. He had it all worked out, down to children, to where we would live. If it hadn't been for Covid, I might have sleepwalked into a marriage and expected a party and a big frock to have done the heavy lifting in convincing us we'd done the right thing. But after everyone had gone and the marquee was being dismantled, I'd have just looked at him and thought, "Is that it?" You remember that time we were looking at that website of that woman in the print frocks who lives like a 1950s housewife?'

Juliet pulled a face. 'Couldn't forget it, the poor cow. All that pastry-rolling.'

'Well, he even said I wouldn't work after we'd had the kids.'

'Wha-?'

'I tried to say I liked working but of course it's a bit difficult to defend that position when I was always moaning about Gullible and Burnt.'

'I think that's called a lucky escape. Well, two. Ed *and* Gullible and Burnt. Can I ask you a personal question?'

'Well, I don't like impersonal ones, so yes.'

'You've known Ed longer than you've known me, which is why I never asked you. Didn't seem much point, if he was already there.'

'Go on.'

'What was the sex like?'

Ash closed her eyes. 'Oh God...'

'I think that's not "Oh God it was to die for."'

'Well, I hadn't much experience to compare it with.'

'Hmm. Experience isn't always what it's cracked up to be.'

'I liked it to begin with. I mean, it was exciting. The way it is with somebody new.'

'Yup. Until you get used to them. Or really get to know them.'

'Is that how it's meant to be, Jules? Cold, sharp prosecco bubbles and then it goes warm and flat?'

'I don't know. I keep hoping I'm wrong. So I keep trying.'

'The thing is, Ed thought he was good at it. He kept looking for praise, anyway. "That was a belter, Ash, wasn't it?" he'd say. Preening himself.'

'Bloody hell.'

'So I always agreed. It was easier that way. Only right from the get-go, I felt a bit short-changed.'

'Like, is that it?'

'Yeah. But I thought it would get better. It didn't.'

'It doesn't. A sex toy is more of a guarantee. Puts you in charge.'

'Oh... I don't know. Feels a bit like cheating.'

'*Ash!* People used to think that about internet dating. What you did if you couldn't meet a guy "normally,"' said Juliet, tracing apostrophes in the air. 'And now it's *the* normal way. Give yourself a break.'

'I think I'm too sensible for my own good, Jules. I've—'

'Hallelujah! We're getting somewhere.'

'What do you mean?'

'No – say what you were going to say before I so rudely interrupted you.'

'Only that I was the same even about going to college. I know I've got my degree and everything, but Business Studies wasn't exactly a fun subject. I chose it thinking it would be easier to get a job, though I know now that you really learn about business by working in it.'

'Maybe. I did Sociology and Criminology but I'd be a hopeless axe-murderess. *Sorry,* interrupting again. Great change of subject, by the way, the college thing.'

'What if I'd done something I really enjoyed? I could have done Italian, even. I'd have had a year abroad and I wouldn't be relying on an App on this trip we're going on. But because I'd never been to Italy the idea never crossed my mind. And now it's too late.'

'For what? Remind me how old we're supposed to be, Ash. I thought it was twenty-eight.'

'I'm scared to go for a new relationship for the same reason. Fear of the unknown. I mightn't be any good at it.

What? What's that look for?'

'Listen to your auntie Jules, Ash.'

'Listening.'

'Never mind another sodding relationship. Have a better one with yourself first. I mean, look at you. You're really pretty. You've a skin to die for – mine's already died under the slap, you see – and a great figure. You go in and out in all the right places. You should see me trying to pour myself into my Spanx of a morning.'

'But—'

'Stop being a doormat, Ash. Stop being afraid of the world and grab it by the bollocks instead. It's like you're even afraid of looking sexy. It was always easier getting dressed for work, wasn't it? You'd those great vintage finds but you hardly ever plucked up the courage to wear them.'

Ash nodded. 'I'm more like poor Cora that I realised.'

'So you need to start dressing for you – the you that you could be. Want another one?'

'No, I'm good.'

'Got your Oystercard with you?'

'Of course.'

'Come on, then, Portobello Road awaits. I don't suppose we can compete with elegant Venetian women, but we can at least look original. And then we could go and find you a sex toy.'

'Omigod. Wouldn't that mean going to some sleazy sex shop? Can't I just buy one online?'

'Chicken. But do I look as if I hang around sleazy sex shops? Seriously, the place I was thinking of is really just a fancy underwear shop with knobs on.'

'Knobs?'

The two of them collapsed into hysterical laughter, enough to attract the attention of the sleek young waiter.

'Glad you're enjoying our coffee so much,' he said with a huge smile. 'Can I get you a refill?'

'You see?' said Juliet a few minutes later, checking her mascara in a hand mirror. 'So many more fish in the sea, Ash – or in the Venetian lagoon, anyway.'

Chapter Six

Stansted

14th April 2022

'You take the window seat,' said Juliet.

'Are you sure?'

'I'll have it on the way back.'

'I don't even want to think about the way back,' said Ash, settling into her seat and clipping the safety belt closed.

'You mightn't have to,' said Juliet. 'Not if you have your wicked way with Dog Man. Oh, what's happened to the magazine?'

'It's Ryanair, remember. And anyway, you don't get magazines even in doctors' waiting rooms these days.'

A prerecorded woman's voice with an Irish accent warned them the flight safety demonstration was about to begin.

'I've missed even the cabin crew doors to manual stuff, Jules. I really do need to get a life.'

The hotel was only five minutes' walk from the stop, on the Lista di Spagna, up a steep flight of steps above a shop selling carnival masks. Ash's initial disappointment that they hadn't been given a room at the front of the building, where the windows had those pretty ogee arches, turned to relief when she realised that though they didn't have a view (a narrow alleyway, a brick wall and a lamp bracket were all that was on offer) they also didn't have the noisy crowds making their *passeggiata* between the station and the Campo San Geremia. Prim twin beds faced them, with a painting of coy angels hanging above. But it was simple, clean and cheap and the lady at reception had been friendly.

'What say you to having a shower, putting on our finest and seeing if we can find someone to give us *spaghetti alle vongole*?' said Juliet.

'No prosecco?'

Juliet put on a pretend wounded expression. 'What do you take me for?'

'Where'll we go, then?'

Juliet's thumbs flicked rapidly on her phone. 'Here's a good one, about fifteen minutes' walk from here. Their menu here says their vongole are *veraci,* whatever that means.'

'Voracious?'

'They're clams, Ash. Anyway, it says "with indoor seating and outdoor terraces, you can enjoy gorgeous views from every table." Only, they aren't really terraces. Just seats outside. There's a button – I could book it now.'

'What's the gorgeous view of?'

'Campo Santa Maria Formosa. Where else?'

'Omigod.'

'No, oh-get-a-shower. We've only got two weeks, remember? And tonight we'll be starring in that webcam ourselves.'

'I can't believe we're really here!' said Ash, gazing across the square she had seen so many times on-screen.

'Hey, kid, we've earned it.' Jules leaned into her friend, squeezing her arm. 'But stop wobbling. If we do meet Dog Man, remember he has no idea who you are.'

'It'll show in my face,' said Ash. 'He'll know I've been stalking him for months!'

'Daft mare... This place looks much bigger than it did on the webcam, doesn't it?'

'And busier – in a good way,' said Ash, swerving as a little girl on a scooter tore past. 'I wonder who is watching us now?' she said, looking up at the gleaming white façade of the hotel at the end of the square.

Juliet waved at it. 'Yoo-hoo!'

'*Stop it!* That man is staring at us.'

'Man? Where? Have him washed and brought to my tent. Oh, *that* man. Oops. I think he might be our waiter. We'll need to make friends with him. He could help with our stake-out.'

'Sink hole, open up,' said Ash, her hand over her face.

But she let Juliet lead her over to the tables underneath the fluttering awnings, reminding herself that after all, it was eight o'clock on a balmy April evening, they were in Venice, and there was a good chance she would never have to devise a marketing strategy again in her life. Figuring out what she might do instead could wait a few days.

And close up the waiter really was worth looking at, even with his nose and mouth covered by the regulation mask. He was slender. His sleeves were rolled up, exposing golden skin and silky dark hairs Ash wanted to reach up and stroke. A little badge bore the name Davide. Ash remembered that in Italian every syllable was pronounced. She rehearsed saying it in her head: *Dah-vi-deh*.

'*Il nome è* Ashworth,' pronounced Juliet carefully.

'Oh yes. You booked,' he said, in nearly unaccented English. 'Your table is here. And you'll find the menu with this Q-R code,' he added, indicating a laminated little square. 'Or I could just tell you…'

'Oh yes, just tell us. It's so good to deal with a real human. What does *vongole veraci* mean?'

Ash saw his eyes smile. 'It means they are unique, the only one. An Italian clam. In this case freshly gathered from the Venetian lagoon. You wish *spaghetti alle vongole*?'

'I do,' said Juliet. 'Ash?'

'Same for me,' said Ash, wishing her blush would subside.

'And to drink?'

'Prosecco? And we'd better have some water. One still, one sparking, Ash?'

Ash nodded, still trying to pull herself together.

'Of course,' said Davide. 'Ladies, if there is anything else you want, just wave to me.'

'He wouldn't need to say that twice,' muttered Juliet, as the waiter moved away.

Ash thought he probably wouldn't either. Davide had been polite to both of them, but she had clocked how his brown eyes kept turning back to Juliet. She suffocated a twinge of jealousy, reminding herself that they had come here, to this square, to find the man with the dog for her. And didn't the best friend in the world deserve a handsome waiter? Especially, she thought as she watched him disappear into the restaurant, one with such an appealing bum.

'I like his arse,' whispered Juliet.

'*He* likes *you*,' said Ash.

'This is meltingly good,' said Ash. 'The spaghetti is just *al dente* and the clams *do* taste real. They taste of the sea.'

Juliet lifted the bottle out of the clinking ice bucket and refilled their glasses.

'I could live like this,' she said.

'Me too,' sighed Ash. Good food, the dryness of the sparkling cold wine against her palate and being with her bestie in the most beautiful city in the world were starting to have their effect. It was as if she could feel herself uncoil.

True, Covid still lurked in the shadows. Masks had to be worn on the vaporetto and in shops – the smaller ones obliged customers to wait outside. She knew museums would require them to show their vaccination certificates, but in every sense Ash felt she could breathe more easily. Residual caution and pre-travel testing meant that Venice was not as busy as she had thought it might be. She was relieved they'd decided to come now. When all restrictions were relaxed Venice might turn into a bear garden. She also realised that if they never even saw Dog Man, it mightn't even matter that much. She was going to have a great time anyway.

Then Juliet said, 'Well, you *might* get to live here. Which door is Dog Man's?'

'There. Right opposite,' she said, pointing across the square.

'What, that posh palace where they've put the lights on deliberately so's we can see in and be jealous?'

'No. I think it's the normal looking building next door. The one with three doorbells. You can only really see the edge of those houses on the webcam.'

'Have you been watching the doors?'

'I haven't, to be honest,' said Ash. 'I've been too busy trying to eat spaghetti without getting it all down my front. I wouldn't want him to live in that palace. It'd be just too much like an old-fashioned rags to riches romance.'

'Well, do you want to hear Baldrick's cunning plan?'

Before Ash could say, 'On the way home, maybe,' Davide reappeared at the table.

'Would you like anything else, ladies?'

'I think I'd like just a green salad,' said Juliet with a virtuous air. 'Remember what we said about eating healthily after Covid, Ash?'

'Not a tiramisu, then?' said Davide.

Ash and Juliet exchanged glances, then Ash said, 'We're on holiday. So we'll have two green salads and afterwards two tiramisus.'

Davide laughed. 'I like that you are such friends, that you even choose the same food. It must be hard to separate you.'

Ash again noticed that when he spoke he was looking at Juliet. *There needs to be a cunning plan for Jules too, not just me. What's wrong with a holiday romance – or more?*

By about ten o'clock they noticed that only one other table was occupied. Ash and Juliet were savouring the *digestif* they'd been offered on the house, a herby, deliciously bitter concoction Davide said was made from artichokes, 'against the strain of modern life,' something that sounded to Ash like a quote. 'You can drink it also as an aperitif,' he said. 'Come at lunch time and try it in the sunshine.'

'Oh, we'll definitely come again,' said Juliet. Ash knew by now that coming back was part of the Cunning Plan that Jules had explained over the tiramisu, but she was glad to see in the look her friend exchanged with the handsome waiter, that there was likely to be a collateral advantage to Juliet too.

Finally, they got up to go. Ash thought for a moment Juliet was going to go on tiptoes and kiss Davide. It wouldn't have been the first time she'd done so with a waiter. But he was already leaning over the table, rolling up the cloth, and gave them only a fond but professional wave.

The girls had almost reached the façade of the church, ambling along arm in arm in the lamplit soft darkness, hearing the gentle lap of water against the hulls of the boats moored in the nearby canal, when they heard Davide's voice cry out in greeting.

'*Ehì*, Gianni! *Come va?*'

Ash knew what she was going to see before she turned round. There was Davide, their tablecloth still bunched in his hands, standing by the well-head talking to another man.

Around them scuttled a small, excitable dog.

Chapter Seven

In a hotel near the station

'It's a sign,' said Juliet, staring up at the shadowy ceiling.

Ash lay in a similar position in the bed alongside her friend's. It was after midnight, but she felt too wired to sleep.

'Not really. He lives there and the dog needed a pee.'

'Our first night, though. Davide knows him and now you've got a name. I can already see you in the Shirt and Shotbag, introducing him to everyone. "This is my boyfriend Gianni. We met in Venice, you know? Yeah, life after Covid!"'

'Stop it!'

'So what did you think of him?'

'I didn't, really. We only caught a glimpse of him. A bit serious, maybe. Nothing wrong with him, though.'

'"Nothing wrong with him, though." Don't suppose he'd want that on his tombstone,' said Juliet.

'That reminds me. What about that trip to the cemetery island? Everybody's buried there: Diaghilev, Stravinsky,

Joseph Brodsky…'

'So where do they put the Italians then? Sounds like the place is full up with Russian dancers. I didn't know you were into ballet.'

'Brodsky was a poet. There are lots of things I used to be into. I'll have you know I was a star pupil at Elite Dance on the Maldon Road when I was twelve. I was going to be the new Darcey Bussell. Even if it wasn't Covent Garden, I loved it.'

'Why did you stop, then?'

'Oh, you know. Being sensible. More time for schoolwork.' Ash sighed.

'That explains it,' said Jules.

'Explains what?'

'Those cheesy photographs they used to take – you know, on training courses, at Sales Conference – when we used to go to the Kingston Doubletree and get death by Powerpoint in person. Most people in them look about as graceful as a sack of coal. But you always managed to be really poised, but like it was easy for you; something about the way you placed your feet. Just like a ballet dancer.'

'Aw, Jules, that's a lovely thing to say! I never realised.' Ash had a sudden vision of the closing night dinner at Sales Conference, back in 2019, her colleagues flailing about on the checkerboard dancefloor, Rupert Brant doing his party-piece, 'John Travolta, 1976!' as if it was something original. Watching from the edge, a glass of Chardonnay warming in her hand, she'd thought the whole thing a bit cringeworthy, but wishing all the same she could let go and behave like an idiot too. She'd only put down her glass and joined the throng when it looked like Joe Mannion was approaching her – something she felt a twinge of meanness about now, remembering how he'd wanted to tell her something that evening on Hampstead Heath. She'd not been encouraging, and then Wanda Brant, of all people, had turned up and whisked him away.

'Anyway, stop changing the subject, Ash.'

'What?'

'We weren't talking about bone islands. We were talking about Gianni.'

'Sorry, I was miles away.'

'Well, not now you are. We're in Venice and we're going back to have lunch at Davide's. That's when Gianni comes out with the dog, isn't it?'

'Tomorrow? We don't need to rush it, do we?'

'You mightn't, but I do. I want to see Davide again.'

Davide was delighted to see them again and made a great fuss about where to seat the two girls. Ash put the menu down the moment he'd scuttled off.

'Jules…'

'Chosen already?'

'Homemade pasta with scallops and Treviso red chicory—'

'Don't know that I've ever eaten chicory. Gran used to go on about something called Camp Coffee that was made with it. Maybe they serve it in places like the Admiral Duncan with a name like that but I don't suppose Gran ever went to a gay bar in her life. Remember that night we went with Fred and his boyfriend when they had the drag act?'

'I do,' said Ash, smiling. 'Jules—'

'Whassup?'

Ash leaned forward and lowered her voice. 'Look where Davide has put us. You're facing towards the church – fair enough. But he moved the other chair around so that I'm at right-angles to you, not facing you but straight opposite that doorway. Gianni's doorway. No – don't look round.'

Juliet of course had done exactly that. Her head snapped back immediately.

'We're being watched!'

Ash rolled her eyes. 'We *were* being watched. I saw him up at the window as soon as we sat down. But he's gone now. He went as soon as your head turned.'

'Oh. Is that creepy, Ash, or is it just me?' said Juliet.

'I can't say it's creepy, can I? Not after I've been watching him for months.'

'He shouldn't have looked away though. A romantic hero in a book would've bowed and smiled and blown us a kiss.'

'That would've been mega-creepy. Anyway, it's not the kind of thing he'd do,' said Ash.

'How do you know?'

'I don't really, only he just looks like a nice, normal guy – from what we saw last night. That hand-kissing stuff is for medallion men. Or Bridgerton heroes.'

'Do you think Davide— Oh, hello! Yes, we are ready to order...well, that is, Ash wants the one with Camp Coffee and I...oh, just a minute.'

'Camp Coffee?' said Davide, a puzzled frown on his handsome face. 'I can bring you coffee, only usually in Italy we serve it after a meal—'

'Only never a cappuccino,' said Ash. 'At most a *caffè macchiato.*'

Davide's face cleared. 'You've done your homework! We never understand why our British visitors want to load their stomachs with a milky drink after they've had a rich meal. It takes away the taste in the way that a simple espresso doesn't. There are local variations, of course. I used to have a girlfriend from Turin. They have something they call a *pousse caffè* in their dialect. It's another glass of wine *after* the coffee. Here it'd be a grappa of course.'

'Have you a girlfriend now?' asked Juliet.

Ash closed her eyes, though she was relieved by the renewed confirmation that the old Jules was back on form. Davide, however, took the question in his stride.

'I am on the market,' he said, smiling. 'Are you offering?'

'*Davide! Sbrigati!*' came a voice from the doorway.

'Oops. That's the boss, telling me to hurry up.'

'Oh, right. Well, Ash is having the homemade pasta with the scallops and I'll go for the spaghetti with cuttlefish. What if we let you choose the wine?'

Davide nodded, scribbling on his pad. *'Va bene.'*

'Oh dear, that was awkward,' said Jules, the moment Davide was out of earshot. The two of them collapsed into giggles. But when Ash got her breath back, she asked, 'So, "do you think Davide" what, Jules?'

'Told Gianni to stand at his window, of course.'

'Ah!'

'It explains why he made you sit where you are. It would help him if Gianni hooked up with you if he wants to hook up with *me,* and...' Jules looked at her friend meaningfully.

'It means that Gianni is unattached too,' said Ash slowly.

'Bingo!'

'Vino!' chimed in Davide, appearing at their table and proceeding to uncork a chilled bottle of Bianco di Custoza. He poured a tasting amount into Juliet's glass and waited.

Juliet swirled the liquid and looked up at him.

'Go on,' she said. 'I trust you.'

With a slow smile Ash could sense even with half his face covered by the mask, Davide filled her glass and followed with Ashley's. Then just as he left them, Ash saw his eyes flick upwards towards the window where she'd seen Gianni earlier. She forced herself not to look too.

The two friends clinked glasses. 'It's happening,' said Jules.

'It is,' said Ash. 'And we're going to have company, probably over coffee. Don't let me drink too much, Jules.'

'Don't worry. I'll soak it up for you. As long as you see me home afterwards. I think it might be worth giving this siesta thing a go.'

Chapter Eight

15th April 2022

'Hey, Killer!' called Davide.

Sitting at their table finishing their coffee, Ash and Juliet exchanged glances. Davide was two tables away, bending over to stroke the soft ears of a shaggy little white dog.

'He doesn't look like a killer,' said Ash nervously. 'And who'd give their dog a name like that?'

'We're about to find out.'

Davide was leading a man over to their table. 'Meet Gianni. We've been best friends since *prima elementare* – since we were six.'

Ash looked up into the face of a kind-looking but somewhat anxious young man, who put out his hand and smiled nervously.

'I'm Ashley. This is *my* best friend Juliet. Only we're late starters. We didn't meet until we were twenty-four.' *Stop gabbling!* 'But you can call me Ash.'

'Ash,' he repeated, puzzled.

'I know. Only in England it was the most popular baby name for girls the year I was born. Mum's always played safe.'

'Played safe?'

Ash grasped that Gianni's English wasn't quite as idiomatic as his friend's. *But Davide has to speak English every day. I wonder what Gianni does for a job?*

'What is it you do?' she said. *Oh for fart's sake, Ash. Sounds like you're checking to see if he's husband material.*

'What do I do?' Gianni looked around as though he was searching for something. 'I take Killer for a walk.'

Ash shut her eyes momentarily, mainly so that she couldn't see the look on Juliet's face.

'Ash means your job,' said Davide. He pointed out the hotel at the end of the square. 'Gianni's a big shot. He's head of IT and maintenance in that swanky place. You can barely see it from here, but if you look carefully, there's a webcam up there that Gianni got installed. So when you have to go home...' Davide paused, theatrically brushing an imaginary tear from his eye. 'You'll be able to watch me at work and Gianni walking Killer and we'll not even know you're there.'

Ash felt heat flood her face.

'Why's he called Killer?' asked Juliet quickly. The little dog went into an appealing hind legs routine at the mention of his name. Ash bent over to make a fuss of him, mouthing silently, 'Thank you, Killer! Thank you, Jules,' relieved to hide her burning face.

'My girlfriend gave him that name, because when he was a puppy he'd try to bite her ankles.'

'Your sort-of girlfriend,' added Davide.

'*Sì*,' said Gianni, as Ash straightened up, glad she wasn't the only person to feel embarrassed. 'We are a little one day yes, one day no.'

'On and off,' said Ash sympathetically. *I like him,* she thought, *the way I like my little brother.*

'Yes. Like a light switch.' She felt guilty, remembering watching Gianni and the on and off girlfriend arguing by the well-head. She'd watched them in dismay, not because they were fighting, but because the girl's presence meant there was no space for herself. Now, looking at Gianni's gloomy expression, she realised that the person she should have felt sorry for was him.

'I've been in that situation,' she said.

Gianni looked at her gratefully. Out of the corner of her eye she could see Davide watching them. *That's friendship for you. He's for Gianni like Jules is for me. Always in my corner, no matter what. Only do I want to be set up with Gianni? He's so sweet, but he's not exactly the thunderbolt I wanted. But I ought to give him a chance – just to stop feeling like a complete idiot.*

Davide took over, bringing a chair over from a now empty table. '*Siediti,* Gianni. Another coffee, anyone?'

Gianni obediently sat down next to Ash. 'Yes, please. Ash?'

Ash nodded. *Gianni's a nice guy. Why not?* 'But decaff, please.'

'I'll have that *pousse caffé* thing,' said Juliet. 'But are you allowed one too?'

Davide scanned the tables. There were only two still occupied.

'I'll check with the boss – and see if Francesco will cover for me.'

'I hope so,' said Juliet. 'You don't want to leave a girl to drink alone, do you?'

Ash felt her face heat up again. Jules never did do subtlety.

Nor it turned out, did Gianni.

Chapter Nine

15th April 2022 - afternoon

An hour later, Ash said, 'I need to decompress a bit.'

'Yes, you look as if you do,' said Juliet. 'Come on then.'

They got up from the table, which had already been stripped. Around them, chairs were tipped forward. Everyone else had long gone – Gianni back to work. Up at a window a disconsolate Killer looked down on them. Juliet took Ash's arm.

'Where are we going? Back for that siesta?'

'I'm too wired now for sleeping, Ash, in spite of all that food. What about you?'

'I'm feeling a bit ... torpid, to be honest,' said Ashley.

'Torpid?'

'I think if I went to sleep now I mightn't ever wake up again. I'd rather have a walk. Where's Davide?'

'Let's get some culture, then. Davide is eating with the others. He said he only has one main meal in the day – a late lunch when all the tourists have finished. There's no time once the evening diners come. Sorry, Ash.'

'What for?'

'For sloping off with him for a tour of the kitchen.'

'Is *that* what you were doing?'

'Not really. But I did get to meet the cook. And the boss. I've learned quite a lot about food, besides eating it.'

'If we go on at this rate we'll not fit on the plane. But I didn't really think you'd sloped off anyway. Davide looked pretty determined to leave Gianni and me alone. Why are you looking like that?'

'I got some of the low down on Gianni's love life,' said Jules. 'He's been with Donatella since middle-school.'

'Yes… that's what he told me. Oh God, talk about too much detail.'

'Hell. I should have rescued you. Only, being kissed in the staff toilet is more romantic than you'd think.'

'Already?'

'I wish. But he has asked for my number. So, what did Gianni have to say for himself?' asked Jules.

'Oh God, where do I begin? Well, he's not with Donatella anymore, according to him.'

'That's a start. Does he want to be?'

'I don't think so. Only …'

'Only what?'

'Um, let me tell you the whole story first. I've a theory, but it's a wild one. First off, Gianni likes to talk about himself.'

'Oh dear.'

'I don't mean in an Ed way - look at me aren't I brilliant. I mean in a poor me I feel really sorry for myself and so should you sort of way.'

'Didn't he ask about you at all?'

'Well, he said I'm a good listener. Perhaps he never gets a word in edgeways with Donatella. It certainly looked that way on the webcam. But I'm really not good at listening at all. I'd to plaster on a fake-concerned expression. My face is still stiff from the effort, and my toes have developed bicep muscles from all the curling and uncurling I was doing under the table.'

'He never told you what that row was about, did he?'

'I was that close to asking him, Jules. Thank Christ I didn't, since I'm not supposed to know about it. But I know why they split up. Donatella thinks he's not ambitious enough.'

'Is that a bad thing? After Ed, I mean?'

'For me you'd think it wouldn't be. But after listening to him for an hour I can sort of see her point. It all started before Covid, you see. There was a guest at the hotel, the kind who was *really* demanding. Asking for weird things at weirder times. Finding fault. Why was Venice so scruffy. Why don't they serve tea with milk. You name it. Anyway, he had some kind of IT problem and Gianni was hauled in to fix it for him. The way this glitch was, Gianni thought it was some kind of set-up. A sort of deliberate perverse ingenuity.'

'I wonder how you say that in Italian?'

'No idea, but it took Gianni a while to explain all of this to me anyway. His English is really good, but not as good as Davide's. Not that I should complain – my Italian is rubbish. There was a lot of Google Translate going on because Gianni had to make sure I'd got it, though I was doing my best not to yawn. Anyway, the executive summary is that this guest from hell was a mystery shopper. He told Gianni – after offering him a job because he saw really quickly through this manufactured IT glitch – that he worked for one of those international hotel chains. Ultra high-end stuff, the kind where you pay a thousand quid just for the pillow. They've no presence in Venice, and this man's task was to find places they could make offers for that just couldn't be refused. Gianni's hotel is a bit small for their usual business model, but it was being considered for some sort of boutique line they're starting, with some name like Portfolio at Fairview, or The Collection.'

'I know the kind of thing,' said Juliet, drily. 'Where they call the punters residents instead of guests even if they're just there for a weekend to fuck the secretary. Yup, been there, done that. Not one of my prouder moments.'

'You never told me about that,' said Ash in admiration.

'I'll put it in my memoirs. The complimentary slippers fell apart pretty quickly but I think I'm still working through all the bathroom stuff I pinched.'

'And the man?'

Jules shuddered theatrically. 'Don't ask. So, didn't Gianni want the man's job? Sounds like quite a good deal. The hotel gets new owners and probably new management if the fellow's standards weren't met, and he gets to stay put.'

'That was the problem. They wanted him to learn the Fairview way.'

'What, like joining the Scientologists, only with minibars and spas and manicurists?'

'Kind of,' said Ash. 'But it wouldn't be here. He'd have to work a couple of years first in one of their flagship destination hotels.'

'What's a destination hotel when it's at home?'

'It's one where the point of your holiday is to go to that particular hotel.'

'Too much money and not enough imagination, in other words,' said Jules. 'Where was this destination hotel going to be?'

'Dubai. It did sound like a good deal. They would even have found a job for Donatella. She's a beautician.'

'Well, she can keep her hot wax to herself.'

'That's why they split up.'

'What, because she wouldn't have a Brazilian or because she did have one?'

'We didn't quite get into *that* much detail, Jules. No, I mean they split up because he turned the job down. Gianni thought he wouldn't hear anything else about it because

Covid got to Italy three weeks after the mystery shopper. But the offer came a couple of months after Venice went into lockdown, wrapped up in some big story about the new dawn and the company's strategic mission for the post-Covid world.'

'Rupert Brant went to work for them, did he? Sounds just like his kind of chin music.'

'Gianni of course had gone and told Donatella about fixing the PC and how he got offered the job on the spot. She got high as a kite about it, how it was going to transform her career as well as his. Gianni warned her it mightn't come to anything. He said it might just have been the fellow swaggering about the place – he hadn't given him anything in writing. But then a twenty-page contract arrived by email, at a time when it looked like the world was going to end, and he got into a complete panic, turned it down without telling her and she went ballistic.'

'I would have too, Ash, even if I hadn't wanted to go to Dubai. On principle. They're supposed to be a couple and he makes a unilateral decision.'

'Gianni is as different as he could be from Ed, but that's who he reminded me of when he said what he'd done.'

'Yup, my thoughts entirely, hun. But did he tell you why he turned it down?'

'This is where I thought he was really sweet – and principled. The first thing he said was that he didn't want to leave Killer behind. Him and Donatella would have been in hotel accommodation – or accommodation owned by the hotel, I'm not sure which. Only not dog friendly.'

'Aw!'

'The other thing he did was to tell his boss what had happened. That really put the fox in the hen-coop. It's still a family-owned hotel though I don't think the family actually have anything to do with the day to day running of it. In other words, it's independent. The word of course went out around all the hoteliers in Venice that Fairview were on the snoop. For some that's about being forearmed, for others it puts them in a better negotiating position if they do want to sell. Gianni of course is the hero of the hour except with Donatella. To be fair, he did go through the entire contract and there was nothing in it that would guarantee he'd get back to Venice with Fairview. He'd also be unlikely to get back into the independent hotel sector here again if he jacked up Dubai partway through. He'd be seen as Judas – his boss is current president of the local chapter of the Veneto hotel federation.'

'As far as that goes, good on him. So, what was your wild theory?'

'I'm probably completely wrong, and Davide is a really nice guy and everything ...'

'Spit it out.'

'I just wondered if maybe I wasn't being set up. You know, Gianni wants to get Donatella back and making her jealous is one way of doing it.'

'Hmm. That would work, only I don't think Davide has anything to do with it. I'm pretty sure he'd like to see the back of Donatella. If he's set this up it's because he really does want his friend to break with her. He thinks Gianni's a bit trapped, and not just because of her.'

'Worse places to be trapped in than Venice, I should think,' said Ash. 'A good reason for turning down Dubai.'

'Davide told me that the population here is dropping like a stone,' said Juliet. 'There won't be any actual Venetians left soon if it goes on like this. The way he put it, it'll be like a big theme park full of Air BnBs. The problem Gianni has, according to Davide, is that he's never really budged. That flat he lives in belonged to his grandparents. His Mum and Dad are separated and his Dad is on the mainland – in Padua – with a new family. His Mum lives in Castello district. He studied at the Ca' Foscari, the University of Venice – did IT. Davide says Gianni has occasionally thought about going somewhere else but it would have been expensive finding another place to live, he doesn't like cars anyway, and possibly he just can't be bothered.'

Ash rolled her eyes.

'I got the impression Davide feels a teeny bit resentful,' Juliet went on. 'Like Gianni has had things easier than him. But he's loyal. They've been friends forever, as you know. Davide didn't tell me about the Dubai thing but my guess is that he would approve of his reason for turning it down, only he probably wishes Gianni had tried working somewhere else for a while, if not perhaps so drastically far away, same as he has had to do. Davide did say that both him and Gianni would feel guilty if they left permanently. Two more Venetians gone away. But it is a bit weird, isn't it? Not only has Gianni never left home, but he's got a job in a hotel he can see from his window.'

'Beats a commute on the Northern Line,' said Ash.

'I'm quite sure when I'm next on it I'll picture him walking from his front door and a minute later into the hotel and think he had the right idea all along.'

'Me too. But what's that about Davide wanting to see the back of Donatella?'

'I think he doesn't like her very much but is too much of a friend to say so,' said Juliet. 'He said he hoped Gianni would find someone better suited to him. But it looks as though Gianni has blown it with you anyway.'

'I'm not sure there was anything to blow anyway.'

'Steady on.'

'Stop it, you!' said Ash, laughing in spite of herself.

'Will you go on watching him?' asked Juliet. 'On the webcam?'

Ash hesitated. 'No. No I won't. And if Gianni thinks I might be right for him I'd be really surprised. He didn't find out a darn thing about me and I never got a word in edgeways. I'll look out for Davide instead, only not in the same way. I'll be thinking about a holiday I'll never be able to forget.'

'If you do,' said Juliet slowly, 'I don't want you to tell me if you see him chatting up other women.'

'Oh Jules… I do think he really likes you…'

'But?'

'No buts.'

'No harm in a holiday romance, is there? Especially after all we've been through. Gran and everything…' Juliet rummaged in her bag. 'Sorry, I…'

'Don't be sorry. My old aunt used to say that every tear you shed for a person you lost gets them closer to heaven,' said Ash.

'I like that. Only I wonder where they go while they're waiting to get in? Do you think it's a bit like Charing Cross Accident and Emergency on a Saturday night?'

'Maybe, but without the drunks.'

'Don't they have something called ambrosia in heaven?'

'I think that's the Greeks. God's probably teetotal,' said Ash.

'Oh, what it is to have a classical education.'

'What, at Moulsham High? I found that out on Wiki when I was looking for something else.'

'We could go to Greece next year and make do with ouzo or something instead. I've never been. My Aunt Ethel is always going on about those Greek millionaire romances.'

'I didn't know you had an Aunt Ethel,' said Ash.

'Porky. Latisha at the hairdresser's passes them on to me. Maybe they're billionaires anyway, what with inflation.

You won't tell everyone on Twitter I read them, will you?'

'Schtum. And I'd love to go to Greece with you. My next Webcam stalk!'

Chapter Ten

What's new on the Rialto?

Ash and Jules leaned on the Istrian stone balustrade, looking down at the chugging vaporetti, the water taxis, the barges and the occasional gondola filled with orderly Japanese tourists passing underneath them.

'It's almost hypnotic, isn't it?' said Juliet. 'I could watch those boats for hours.'

'Just like our seagull. He's still there.'

'Do you think he's the same one?'

'Dunno. Don't know enough about seagulls. But maybe they have territories, like cats.'

Another gondola passed beneath them, this time with a middle-aged couple entwined on the red cushions. Ash felt tears prick her eyes. They looked so happy.

Echoing her thoughts, Jules said, 'Look at them. There's hope for us too if we hang around long enough. It's just a question of patience.'

'I wonder what their story is. I wonder if that's a

honeymoon or a wedding anniversary.'

'Or neither. Perhaps they're both married to other people,' said Juliet.

Then Ash remembered that there had been a married man. Jules hadn't said a great deal about him, except that she'd been about eighteen and him twenty-nine, a bigger gap then than had Jules been twenty-nine and the man forty. He'd made all kinds of promises he'd no intention of keeping. 'I wish I'd known you back then, Ash,' Juliet had told her. 'I needed the kind of friend who'd love me, no matter what.'

Standing there on the bridge, Ash said nothing, but put her arm around Juliet's shoulders. Jules hugged her back, then said, 'I think we need a bit of therapy.'

'Handbags?'

'Definitely handbags.'

They made their way back onto the central part of the bridge where the shops were, but eventually found the 'bags to die for' not on the bridge itself but on the Ruga d'Orefici on the far side, where there were pretty much the same designs as on the bridge but at more reasonable prices. They bought similar bags but in different colours.

'They've got a real Birkin vibe,' said Ash, putting her hand into the stiff card carrier-bag to stroke the smooth leather. 'Classic.'

'Only without the price tag. Anyone can buy expensive bags if they've the money. *We've* got style and imagination.'

'Have we? I mean, have I? Not like Italians have.'

Jules frowned slightly, thinking. 'It's a question of getting the details right. The right shoes, belts, bags. A good pair of sunglasses. Not overdoing it.' She stopped and stared at Ash. 'I've got it,' she said.

'Got what?'

'I mightn't get another opportunity. You know how I have always loved vintage?'

'We both do,' said Ash, thinking of the Saturday mornings they'd spent in places like the Oxfam Boutique in Westbourne Grove.

'I know about marketing, and web design and all that.'

'Ye-es?'

'And there's my sewing machine. I used to make *lots* of things, when I had more time. And – what is it they call it? Remastering? No, that's records, isn't it?'

'Repurposing. Upcycling.'

'Yeah. Well, it's a bit of a bandwagon now, I suppose. But why not ride the wave?'

'Ride the wave in a bandwagon?'

'OK, mixed metaphors. But you know what I mean. Hell, Ash, I don't want to work the way we were before Covid. I want to do something new. Something I can set up on-line and not be dependent on anyone but myself.'

Ash was startled to hear Juliet's voice shake with emotion. 'Bespoke upcycled clothes. Gran left me her savings. She was somebody who knew how to dress. She'd been a floorwalker in an old-fashioned department store when she was young – Swan and Edgar. I don't know who is in that building now but she couldn't bear to go and see it after Debenham's took over.'

'And now old Debs have got the skids under them. Jules – do it. I've never, ever seen you way excited the way you are now. I only met your nan a couple of times, but I'm sure she'd want you to do this. What was her first name?'

'Everyone called her Lucy, but I've seen her death certificate. Her real name was Lucia. Her Mum was Italian.'

'Lucia. That's the name of your shop, then.'

'Yes!' said Jules, looking as though she was about to dance on the spot. 'I want a gondola too.'

'A *gondola*? You'll not get one of them home on Ryanair.'

'For the logo. I need to design the logo. That'll help me understand what I'm aiming at,' said Juliet, thumbs busy over her phone. 'I need a stationer's first. Says here there's one in Calle San Cassiano. That's just along here. The normal shops should have reopened for the afternoon by now.'

Twenty minutes later Juliet was armed with a small sketchpad and a pack of coloured pencils.

'Now what?' said Ash.

'I'm railroading you again. We were going to do culture this afternoon, weren't we?'

'There's been culture here for centuries,' said Ash. 'It'll

wait for us another couple of days. And no, you're not railroading. I'm just hoping your energy is catching.'

'Window-shopping. That's what I was thinking of. Find out where the designer duds are and sketch them.'

'Or you could just take pictures of them.'

'It's not the same. I want to be inspired by them, to interpret them, not copy them. If I draw pictures of them then I get a better feel for how the clothes are made because I'll be looking at them properly. And if I don't like some detail I can change it in my sketch straightaway.'

'We passed a Luisa Spagnoli shop on the way here. Just the other side of the Rialto.'

'Start there?'

'Yes. But don't forget there's a Gucci in the Fondaco dei Tedeschi and some other high-end names. And all those swanky stores on the Calle Larga. But one condition, Jules. The first person you make an upcycled dress for is me.'

'Deal!'

Chapter Eleven

16th April 2022: Ten thousand virgins

'Culture today, isn't it?' said Juliet across the breakfast table the following morning. 'You were organising museums and I was making sure we'd get fed and f—'

'Ssh! Those Germans over there are staring at us again.'

'Just jealous.'

Ash rolled her eyes. 'Well, you were multi-tasking when you found Davide's place. But when – I don't think it's going to be if, after all – you bring him back here, let me know.' She dropped her voice. 'I realise he's got a great bum but I don't want to come back to Room 4 one of these days and it be the first thing I see.'

'You won't,' said Jules confidently. 'You're not allowed to take people into hotel rooms in Italy if they aren't checked in. *If* I get acquainted with Davide's giblets it'll be in his own place, not here.'

Ash prayed that the Germans' probably excellent command of English didn't include potential interpretations of giblets. 'How did you know that?'

'Did my homework. It's a girl scout thing. Being prepared.'

'I never knew you were a girl scout.'

'I wasn't. The uniform was horrible and they didn't have badges for the things I liked doing. But it is *if,* not when. Like I said, I don't want to rush things. We've another week after all.'

Laughing, Ash said, 'I don't know if you're joking or not.'

'I have that problem too. With me, I mean. So, culture?'

'Yup,' said Ash, producing the timed tickets she had booked for the Accademia gallery.

'If they book people like that I suppose that means at least it won't be rammed,' said Juliet.

'It won't be. You'd never be able to maintain social distancing otherwise. We should make the most of it. We'll probably never have Venice so much to ourselves ever again.'

'You're the brainy one, Ash. What should we go and see there?'

'The legend of St Ursula,' said Ash promptly.

'You're kidding? I was educated by the Ursulines.'

'Were you? I'd forgotten you were posh.'

'I think that's why I went off the rails,' said Juliet cheerfully. 'Something to do with being in an all girls school. Even if not very many of the teachers were actually nuns. So what's this legend?'

'Didn't the nuns tell you?'

'Old Sister Goretti was always on about saint stories. I wasn't very good at listening, though the best ones were pretty gory.'

'Come on, then. Finish your coffee.'

'Wow!' said Juliet, looking at the nine vast canvases, hung in a room of their own. 'They're like a great big comic strip.'

'That's exactly what they were,' said Ash, her head bent over her phone. 'It says here they were in the hall of the confraternity of the saint, except for that one of her going up to heaven. That was in their chapel. Ursula was a Breton princess who was supposed to marry an Englishman, only he was a pagan.'

'Aren't most Englishmen these days?'

Ash mimed looking at her friend over a pair of spectacles.

'Go on, I am interested,' said Jules.

'She told her father she wouldn't marry him though, unless he converted and went with her on a pilgrimage to Jerusalem.'

'As you do…'

'See that scene, there, with her counting off her fingers?'

'That her Dad, then? He looks a bit fed up listening to her.'

'She wanted some followers to go with her too.'

'Followers? Like on Insta?'

'Behave!'

'Sorry, Ash. I'm listening. I don't know why I was never told this story at school.'

'Because Ursula insisted on ten thousand virgin handmaidens.'

'*What?*'

'*Silenzio,*' murmured the attendant from a seat in the corner.

'I mean, where would you *find* them all?' whispered Juliet. 'And who would check?'

'It doesn't say anything about that here,' said Ash, her thumbs flicking across her phone.

'Well, you'd never be able to round up ten thousand virgins these days.'

'Probably you couldn't then. Anyway, it says here that the story wasn't taken that seriously even a long time ago and that perhaps there were only eleven handmaids at most. They never saw Jerusalem, however many they were. They got as far as Cologne where they were massacred by the Huns. The poor prince as well.'

'That's them in that painting over there, then. They look really calm. Kneeling and praying and waiting to be shot full of arrows. But the pictures are really beautiful.'

They are, thought Ash, looking at the pennants waving in the breeze, the marbled columns, Ursula's gilded coronet, the rich dresses she and her handmaidens wore. Carpaccio, she noted, hadn't even tried to paint ten thousand girls, or if he had given it a go he'd given up after a couple of hundred, but he had produced a wonderful pageant.

'I'd like a bedroom like that one,' said Juliet, pointing to a canvas where a demure looking Ursula lay asleep as an angel approached. 'I've always liked four-poster beds. You've even got to go up a step to get into it.'

'The angel has come to tell her she'll be martyred,' said Ash.

'So she knew and she went anyway?' Her friend whistled; the attendant cleared her throat loudly. Juliet turned in her direction and mouthed 'sorry,' but the woman's expression didn't change.

'Fast track to paradise, I suppose.'

'"Good girls go to heaven, bad girls go everywhere,"' quoted Juliet.

'Who said that?'

'Meat Loaf, though I don't suppose he thought of it first. Maybe it was Mae West.'

'I remember,' said Ash. 'Oh look, there's a little dog at the foot of the bed. He's not taking any notice of the angel.'

'Not like Killer, then. He'd be yapping at him for a burglar.'

'I think I liked the Carpaccio paintings best,' said Ash later. 'Not just the St Ursula ones. That one in the other room where they're fishing a relic out of the Grand Canal – with all the gondoliers and the chimney pots.' She reached for the second cappuccino of the day, sitting outside in nearby

Campo Santa Margherita. The little bar Juliet had insisted on going to was a simple, old-fashioned looking place, its fascia painted a fading red. There were tourists, but boatmen came and went, drinking espresso standing at the counter and greeting their friends in a dialect Duolingo hadn't prepared Ash for.

'The one with that rickety old Rialto Bridge made out of wood?' said Jules.

'I expect they didn't have so many tourists then.'

'Want another one? I was wondering about those *panini* they've got.'

'Good idea,' said Ash. 'Perhaps we should just make them our lunch. That is, unless Davide is expecting us?'

'Don't think we can afford to eat there every day, hun. Might be an idea to keep him hungry as well. And I have reminded him that this is *our* holiday.'

'Jules… if you want to have time with him that's absolutely OK. I'm not going to be your third wheel. Anyway, look at this place. I could wander around it for hours not talking, just looking. I probably need some thinking time. Still trying to process life after Ed.'

'Regrets?'

'None. I think I like being on my own. I think I'm getting to like me.'

'About time. And not too bothered about getting to like Gianni?'

'He's a really nice guy. But there's no spark.'

'Disappointed?'

'Yeah. Of course I am. And feeling pretty stupid with it. I mean, making a grand pash out of a man I couldn't even see well enough to know if he had a beanie hat on or his own hair.'

'Don't feel stupid. Feel hopeful. You're open to loving again when the time's right.'

'Maybe. But I'm also not sure if I want to take on somebody else's baggage again. All that backstory with Donatella, for instance. I'd like to please me for a bit, not worry about someone else licking his wounds.'

'Gianni likes you. He told Davide so. Davide thinks Donatella isn't good for him but doesn't know how to tell him. It's like she wants them to get married because that's the next thing you do, not because Gianni is in the grip of a big pash of his own. I really think he's trying to put you two together for Gianni's sake, not so's he can get me on his own.'

'If you needed time on your own you have it,' said Ash. 'It's not like we're at a party and please-mind-my-handbag while I go to the loo. I'd be perfectly happy just wandering around this city alone anyway. I feel absolutely safe here.'

Jules pulled a mock-disappointed face. 'Don't you like wandering around it with me, then?'

'Don't be daft. Of course I do. Especially seeing you making those drawings you did yesterday.'

'Omigod, that was so funny when that woman came

out of the Fendi shop in Calle Largo San Marco yesterday wanting to know what we were doing.'

'Silly cow. As if you couldn't copy the designs in five minutes on the net. But it was worth it from the look on her face when you tore out the page and handed it to her unasked and said, "Bit old for me anyway, dear." I'd only think of the put downs three days afterwards. But back to poor Gianni—'

'I know he hasn't a hope in the world if you call him poor Gianni.'

'Well, he is and he isn't. He's living in what used to be his grandparents' flat, has a job it takes him three minute walk to get to, including walking downstairs, went to university in the same city and eventually he'll probably get married in Santa Maria Formosa the other end of the square from where he works. That's either lucky – live in Venice, no commute, no rent to pay. Or it's a bit scary. Like being in a pen.'

'There are worse pens. It's different for Davide. He *knows* he wants to be here. He told me he had two years in London when he left school, working in a restaurant in Paddington and in a posh hotel – can't remember which one, but I had heard of it. He's still studying, part-time. Whereas Gianni's parents supported him to go to the Ca' Foscari full-time and now he's got a much better job. But Davide said he wanted to see a little bit of the world before deciding if he wanted to be here. So in a way he loves Venice more. He's come back. Whereas Gianni has never bothered to leave it. Am I overanalysing this, Ash?'

'No. But you must see it makes Gianni look less appealing, even if he has got the good job, the flat and all the rest of it.'

'I do.'

'And to be honest, he's a bit of a wet blanket. Killer is a lot livelier.'

'Ow. Well, if it's any comfort, I don't think he's right for you either – Gianni, I mean, not Killer.'

'Whereas Davide could be right for you.'

'Early days...'

'Where is it he lives?'

'He rents a duplex somewhere in the Castello district near his Mum, so he takes his washing home to her on his days off. He says that apart from one old lady all the other apartments in the building he's in are Air BnBs. So he and the old lady do their best to be good neighbours, as the tourists barely give them the time of day.'

'Though I bet they go home and say they stayed somewhere "typically Venetian."'

'Probably.'

Ash looked around the long rectangle of the square where they sat. 'Round here feels a bit more real, though, just a bit less posh than at Santa Maria Formosa. Kids playing, and those guys over there look like students...' She tailed off, staring in disbelief.

'What is it?' said Jules. 'You look like you've seen a ghost.'

'Over there.' Ash pointed at a knot of young men, talking and laughing.

'What?'

'Oh, they're disappearing down that alley. One of them was the dead spit of Joe Mannion.'

'Get away,' said Juliet. 'All I could hear was Italian. Joe doesn't speak Italian.'

'He might. I never thought he liked the Grateful Dead or would have a mural in his flat until we saw him on Zoom.'

'What would Joe be doing here?'

'Haven't the foggiest,' said Ash. 'Those guys looked more like art students than accountants. But then I hadn't the foggiest why Wanda Brant was bossing him around at that thing on Hampstead Heath.'

'A mirage, then. Only don't people usually have mirages about something they really want, like water in the desert?'

'I suppose so,' said Ash.

'Hey, cheer up. If it's not Gianni, there'll be someone else,' said Juliet.

'I *like* Gianni. He's a really nice guy, but it's all too complicated. What if Donatella shows up again?'

'Just donnateller anything.'

Ash groaned.

'Come on, then,' said Jules. 'Guidebook out. Where'll we go after we've eaten those panini?'

'Fancy a boat trip? A bit of sea air?'

Ash and Jules stood near the front of the queue on the landing stage at San Zaccaria, to get the vaporetto to Murano.

'First time I've been on a bus stop that creaks and moves up and down,' said Jules. 'I could probably get used to it though.'

'Beats catching the number 91 to Crouch End,' said Ash, as the boatman unhooked the chain, letting them on to the boat. They quickly got seats in the stern and the boat rumbled off at speed out into the open water before following the line of the Riva degli Schiavoni. Twisting her head round to look back towards the belltower of San Marco, Ash had the impression that it too was a mirage, like seeing the man who looked like Joe Mannion earlier. Venice was one of those immediately recognisable places, even for people who had never been there, so there were moments when seeing it in three dimensions it still looked like an image, not its real self. Turning in the other direction, she saw the serene dome of the church of San Giorgio Maggiore, sitting quietly on its own little island, and felt she had an inkling for the first time of what it was that might make a man or a woman want to retire from the world behind the walls of monastery or convent. *Only I expect these days they have Zoom meetings with their bishop or whoever, same as anyone else. Perhaps they do podcasts too.*

Jules nudged her arm. 'What are you thinking about?' she said, over the roar of the engine.

Because an image from an hour or so earlier came to mind, she said, 'I wonder what Joe's doing now?'

'Stop thinking about him, Ash. Just live.'

'I wasn't thinking about him. It was just seeing that man earlier that looked so like him.'

'Oh, you mean *Joe*. I thought you were talking about Ed. Hard to hear you over the noise.'

'I don't think I've thought about *him* since I got here. That's horrible, isn't it?'

'Nope,' said Jules. 'What would have been horrible is if you'd come here with him instead of me. You'd have been sat in a gondola being photographed by tourists from every little bridge you went under. And then he'd have got out a ring from a plush little box.'

'Oh don't!'

'Only I don't suppose he would have knelt down. It'd be difficult to do that in a gondola. They're so narrow and he might have unbalanced it and sent the pair of you and the poor gondolier into the drink.'

Despite herself, Ash started to laugh.

'We could start there,' said Jules, pointing to the main island of Venice to their left, where buildings ended and what looked like a public park began, lush with trees. 'Living, I mean. I think it's somewhere in there where they hold the Biennale, the big film festival. That would be life, wouldn't it, swanking about in the middle of the afternoon wearing evening gowns with the paparazzi clicking away?'

'I think I'd hate it. That's unless I was wearing a dress *you'd* made,' said Ash loyally.

'Aw, my bestie!'

The boat began its turn in an arc to the left, skirting the edge of what she could see on her map was called the island of Sant'Elena. A bell tower came into view, leaning at an angle like the tower in Pisa. Small, undistinguished apartment blocks were visible through the trees. Ash wondered what it would be like to live there, in an area not thronged with tourists, to be able to walk the dog and go to the shops and never have to look left-right-left – *or right-left-right it would be here, I suppose* – before crossing the road. *But probably hundreds of foreigners have had the same idea before me and had the money to do it. Doesn't mean they should have, though. Otherwise where do the normal people get to live? The ones that want to be there all year round?*

The boat was now travelling along the length of the far side of the main island of Venice, passing alongside the quiet walls and cypresses of the cemetery islet of San Michele. Ash saw the tops of small buildings huddled together, houses for the dead.

'You don't get to stay there for long unless you're rich and famous,' said Jules. 'Ten years and then they dig you up, and provided you've rotted down enough you get put on a shelf or into a bone pit. I read it somewhere.'

'Ugh!' said Ash. 'Only I can see they'd not have the space otherwise. So being in the cemetery is only a kind of waiting room. Hey, like you said, Jules. Let's live first.'

The boat they were travelling on did a circuit after Murano of Torcello and Burano, but for today, Ash and Jules were just going to go to the first of these, the traditional home of Venetian glass-blowing. Ash thought of the elaborate chandeliers she'd seen in the pictures of the hotel where Gianni worked, realising that he'd probably been responsible for putting together the website she'd pored over. She'd settle for a little glass ornament for her Mum, something like a brightly coloured dog with spindly legs and bug-eyes, if what they had in the shops in Venice were anything to go by. Ash's own flat was spartan, clean lines in pale grey and cream and no clutter in sight. By contrast, home, back in Chelmsford – because home is what Mum and Dad's always was, after all – was something of a curiosity shop with figurines on every surface, diligently dusted once a week. The silly, smiling faces of her mother's Doulton pretty ladies irritated Ash, but at the same time they brought fond tears to her eyes.

That evening they met Donatella, who was anything but a simpering Doulton statuette.

Chapter Twelve

Will you marry me?

'I've made a New Year's resolution,' said Jules, linking Ash's arm as they stepped off the gently bucking vaporetto onto the landing stage at the Fondamenta Nuove, to be nearer Campo Santa Maria Formosa. They'd each eaten a generous *Napoli* in Pizzeria Marlin on the island and were now heading for a nightcap with Davide and Gianni.

'But it's not New Year.'

'Doesn't matter. It's the principle that counts. I'm going to start now so that I've got into the habit by Christmas. The next time I go out for a meal I'm going to start it with an *apéritif* and end it with a *digestif*.'

'Like that's going to be hard! So, you're going to add to Don Luigi's Bottomless Prosecco Brunch?' said Ash, naming a pizzeria back home that the two friends sometimes treated themselves to on lazy Sundays.

'Yes, why not do the job properly?'

Ash was silent, falling into step with her friend.

'Penny for them, Ash?'

'They're lovely in there – at Don Luigi's, I mean. But it's not the same as being here.'

'Well, no. Streatham Hill isn't.'

'It's great for Sundays though. Stops you thinking about what's waiting for us on Monday mornings.'

'Not anymore,' said Jules. 'I'm going to book them for the first Sunday we're back so we can celebrate our new direction.'

'You have yours. I don't know mine, Jules. And I should never have thought of Gianni to provide it.'

'How disappointed are you about that?'

Ash squeezed her friend's arm. 'Not. It was pure fantasy. Only I don't know what to put in its place now.'

As they crossed the square to the little knot of tables, Ash saw Gianni get to his feet.

'He's been looking out for us,' muttered Juliet.

'Looks pretty nervous,' said Ash.

'Yup. And there's why,' said Juliet.

The girl at the table was looking both of them up and down, unsmiling.

'Ashley, Juliet, meet my *fidanzata,* Donatella,' said Gianni nervously. Davide hovered inscrutably in the background, but Ash saw he had a clutch of flutes in his hand; a bottle of Prosecco stood ready in a cooler on the table.

Donatella put out a cool hand to each of them in turn,

saying 'pleased to meet you.' Ash thought she looked like anything but. Donatella was one of those women who made her feel awkward at the best of times: slender, with a well-cut dress of fashionably coarse linen of the kind that didn't crease the moment you took it off the hanger, a statement necklace and long impossibly glossy black hair.

'Congratulations on your forthcoming wedding,' said Ash with forced brightness. *Surely that'll make her smile?*

Instead there was an awkward silence. Donatella then made it even more awkward.

'*Veramente*? Gianni has not asked me.'

'Oh... I'm sorry. I thought... *fidanzata*. You know, like fiancée.'

Ash felt deeply sorry for Gianni, for Donatella was ignoring her and looking daggers at him. *Not daggers, more like meat skewers. More painful,* thought Ash.

Davide tried to come to the rescue. '*Fidanzata* is what we say when we mean a serious girlfriend – *fidanzato* for boyfriend. It doesn't necessarily mean they are engaged.'

'*Scusatemi*,' said Gianni, and without another word ran off.

'Gia—?' Everyone else followed Donatella's startled gaze. But Gianni hadn't gone far. He was standing at his own front door, fumbling for keys. He managed to get it open, then rushed in leaving the door ajar.

'He'll be back in a minute,' said Davide. Ash wondered why he was frowning. 'Shall I pour?'

Nobody spoke, but they watched him as he gently eased out the cork with the softest of pops.

'Well done,' said Juliet. 'A proper duchess's fart.'

Donatella stared at her in disgusted astonishment. '*What* did you say?'

'She's just given me a compliment,' said the valiant Davide. 'I remember the farting duchess from London—'

'Who *is* this woman?' demanded Donatella.

Ash could see the effort it took Davide not to roll his eyes. 'There is no woman, Donatella. That is what they called it when I worked at Claridges. Making an explosion with a champagne cork is for boat parties or picnics. The best *sommelier* should withdraw it slowly, slowly...'

Ash heard Juliet stifle a giggle.

'And with the softest "puff." That's why they call it a duchess's fart.'

Donatella looked put out. Ash wondered if she thought she was being made fun of. She was pretty sure the girl didn't like being shown up for not knowing something.

At the moment Davide leaned in to pour, they heard a door slamming. Gianni rushed up, looking flustered, one hand balled into a fist. Ash had the impression he'd brushed his hair but thought it an odd reason to run away from the table.

'Oh yes,' he said breathlessly. '*Un brindisi.*'

Ash had heard of Brindisi. It was a city down south but she'd never thought of going there. Davide caught sight of

her puzzled expression. 'Gianni means a toast,' he explained.
'Gianni?'

Gianni was sinking below eye level. Ash nearly asked,
'Have you dropped something,' but realised just in time
that he was on one knee in front of Donatella, muttering
something of which she could only make out the word *sposa*.

Ash knew what that meant. There was a shop called *Bella
Sposa* in Upminster, near where her auntie Margaret lived. A
bridal boutique. Gianni had opened his fist to reveal a little
box. He pushed in the spring and Donatella leaned forward,
looking like the cat that got the cream. She picked up the
ring and to Ash's astonishment turned it from side to side.
There was what felt like an interminable silence before she
smiled and nodded. With trembling fingers Gianni pushed
the ring onto Donatella's wobbling extended finger. Then
around them, the other diners, forgotten until then, erupted
into cheering and clapping. Ash and Juliet exchanged glances
and joined in. At last Donatella looked happy.

Ash was less sure about Gianni. His expression was a
mixture of resignation and relief.

The two girls were halfway along narrow Calle Trevisana
on their way back to the hotel when Juliet said, 'He hadn't
planned to ask her this evening, had he?'

'No,' said Ash, in a small voice. 'He'd have had the ring
on him if that had been the case. It's all my fault for not
understanding Italian properly.'

Juliet turned and hugged her. 'No it's not. If he hadn't really intended to ask her he'd have just kept the conversation going about the mistakes we make learning foreign languages. That's what Davide was trying to do. And remember, Gianni *did* have a ring, up in his flat. He's probably been trying to get up the courage for ages and you just gave him that last little push.'

'Well, I hope they're happy together.'

'They know what they're getting into, anyway. Are you disappointed, Ash?'

'No, not at all.'

'You didn't want that ring for yourself?'

'*No!*'

They walked on, their footsteps echoing in unison.

'Omigod, her face was a picture when you said that about the duchess's fart!' said Ash eventually.

'Did you see the expression on Davide's face as he pulled out the cork?'

'*Behave!*' said Ash, as they collapsed into giggles.

The next morning a rather subdued Ash and Jules went by emailed arrangement to see some paintings by Carpaccio in the little confraternity building of San Giorgio degli Schiavoni, scenes from the life of St George, St Tryphon and St Jerome, set above wooden panelling in a low-ceilinged room.

'It's like stepping back centuries,' whispered Ash. 'Not like when we were in the gallery looking at Saint Ursula.

You knew you were in a picture gallery then. Here you think the people who paid for these paintings have just left the room.'

'They're smaller, more intimate. That helps,' said Jules, also keeping her voice down. It was early. Miraculously, there were no other people in chamber apart from the attendant who had confirmed their booking.

'Why are we whispering, Jules?'

'Dunno. Just seems right somehow. If I spoke in my normal voice I think I'd disturb some ghosts. Ugh! Look at that,' she added, pointing at the scene where George was charging on a large black horse at the dragon, skewering it through the mouth, his lance coming out through the back of the creature's skull. Roundabout lay skulls, the upper part of a desiccated corpse of indeterminate sex. A young man, more freshly dead, lay stretched on the ground, a leg and an arm chewed away. To the right, a demure looking princess looked on with clasped hands. Ash didn't think she looked a bit like anyone who had been minutes from a ghastly death. In a neighbouring scene St George brought the still living but cowed dragon on a leash into an elegant Renaissance town, his broken lance still stuck in the animal's head. The warrior saint held a sword up, about to finish off his captive before an appreciative crowd of turbaned, richly dressed onlookers.

St Tryphon turned out to be a small boy who appeared to have a dragon of his own.

'It says here that's a basilisk,' said Juliet, who had the guidebook, 'only I'm not sure Carpaccio ever saw a real one.'

But there were real animals and birds in all the paintings: a lithe greyhound, a bright red parrot, a dromedary, a donkey, what Ash thought was a mongoose on a long chain, a peaceful looking lion nevertheless causing some terrified monks to flee in all directions, and best of all, a little woolly dog waiting patiently for his master to write down whatever inspiration was coming at him through the open window of his study.

'He looks a bit like Killer,' said Juliet.

'I wonder if Donatella likes Killer...' mused Ash.

'Were you wanting to adopt him?'

'I think I've more in common with him than Gianni, anyway.'

Jules looked at Ash. 'That's a smile, at any rate,' she said.

'Oh Jules... I've got to get a grip. I can't just wait for things to happen. I feel about as passive as that princess, standing about waiting for a dragon to eat her and not doing anything about it. Then some fellow rides up on a horse with a sharp stick and sorts everything out for her. I don't suppose St George married her too?'

'Doesn't say that here. You never hear about saints getting married. Sister Goretti never mentioned it anyway.' Juliet put a hand on her arm. 'Is that what you wanted?'

'I thought I did. Something like what Mum and Dad had. They met when they were nineteen. But I know now all I was looking for was somebody to make life interesting. Give me some kind of definition - direction. This is scary, Jules! I sound like something out of the 1950s!' Ash started to cry. The attendant looked up from her corner; Ash saw her get up, but then the door was darkened by a swarm of Dutch tourists with their guide. Juliet led the way around the edge of the crowd and they escaped into the morning air.

'This way,' said Jules.

Five minutes later they were sitting in the glittering gloom of Venice's Greek church. They had the place to themselves, sitting on carved seats that lined the walls, leaving the creamy Istrian stone and pink Verona marble floor clear. Incense hung in the air. Ash stared up at the far end of the church, with its wooden screen of shimmering icons.

'It's beautiful!' she said. 'It's like being in another world.'

'I expect they've got places a bit like it in Hendon,' said Jules. 'You know, along with London Greek Radio. Did I ever tell you about Nic the Cypriot?'

'No, but not in here, please!'

'Quite right,' said Jules, not in the least put out. 'That's one to tell over a glass of prosecco – or two. Never mind him anyway. It's you we need to sort out.'

'I ought to be happy here. Well, I *am* happy here, but also not happy as we'll be going back home soon. It was all right, really, when I had that job. I mean I didn't need to think about it too much. The next project would come along, I'd write the copy, organise the photoshoots and the graphics, brief the usual suspects, off the product would go and people would buy it, or not. Then there were the focus groups, before and after. What did they want to see in a campaign. What did they think of the campaign just out. Rinse and repeat.'

'You were good at it.'

'Was I?'

'Don't look so surprised. People liked you too. No Flash Ash.'

'What?'

'No Flash Ash. I heard you called that. You just got on with it without a fuss. Things happened when they were supposed to happen. You were good at getting people to work with each other too. It's because you didn't have that big ego marketing people are supposed to have. Creatives, you, know.' Jules flourished an arm over her hair, tipping her head back. 'I'm really, really surprised they didn't keep you.'

'Why would they? The new people wouldn't know what I was like.'

'True, but Bermuda man ought to have told them. Nobody in the new company will have a clue about how it all hangs together. They'll think they've been sold a pup, whereas financially it was sound. It could have recovered after Covid.'

'Not that Rupert Brant will care,' said Ash slowly.

'Nope. He's got his spondulicks.'

'His what? I didn't know he was ill.'

'He isn't, so far as I know. I've got Nic the Cypriot on the brain, sitting in here. He used that word to mean money. He said it has a Greek origin, a kind of seashell people used to use as currency.'

'I wish I'd lived a bit – the way you have.'

'Stop it. You make yourself sound ancient. And some of that life I could have done without.'

'I liked what you said though, about how I did that job. I never knew. The appraisals I had were always a bit meaningless. A general pat on the back.'

'You were taken for granted, Ash. Thing is, I think *you* take yourself for granted too. So, forget the car ads – we're in Venice after all. I also think you mightn't have been tested enough in that job. Neither of us were. When you said that about 'rinse and repeat' – it was just same old same old.'

'But now what? "Same old same old" in a new place where I don't know anyone? Those temporary contracts are pretty exhausting. I only do them to pay the rent.'

'Then make sure it's something different, Ash. But let's start with what you know. What do you miss about the old job?'

'That's easy. The people. Meaning the staff – you, Nirmala. I wish I'd got to know some of them better – people like Joe even. I'm a bit shy about meeting new people.'

'Well, I'm not going anywhere. What about the clients?'

'Some of them. Not all.'

'List the ones you liked. You're going to be writing to them.'

'Oh, I *couldn't*.'

'Damn well can. They'd jump at the chance of getting you and they are the devil you know. But you're right that you might just be slotting back into the same old same old that way. So what else did you like?'

'Being useful. Setting up systems to work properly – things other people overlooked.'

'Go on.'

'Well, I felt I was useful to individual people, but not that what we were doing was useful in the grand scheme of things. I mean, I know it sounds like heresy but isn't one car pretty much like another one? I mean, the only car contract I worked on that I felt made any sense was that electric one. The others were all boy-toys. The sort of cars that would have a salesman's four pressed shirts hanging up in the back. I'm really envious of you, Jules, with your upcycling idea. And you came up with it when we were looking at handbags. I just feel right now that I've no imagination – except for fantasies about a man I'd seen on a webcam who turned out to be a bit of a damp squib. And now it's my fault he's getting married to someone else.'

'Most men are damp squibs, darling, when you hope they're going to be Roman Candles. Long and hard and then they explode making a lot of noise.'

'Stop it!' spluttered Ash, her shoulders shaking with suppressed laughter. 'Remember where we are!'

'All right, I'll try to behave. Only don't be so tough on yourself. You're good at what you do. I think it's more a case of finding the right people to do it with. You even look the part.'

'Meaning?'

'You always look professional. Very neat, properly turned out.'

'Not like Donatella, then. Just dull.'

'All right, I'd like to look like Donatella too. Effortless elegance and hair to die for. Not curves and curls. But you're not dull, just properly put together. As if you know what you're doing. Not like you've had to rootle something out of the ironing basket five minutes before you've to catch the Tube.'

'I wish I had a bit of the verve they've got here. And your curves and curls are beautiful. I'm sure Davide thinks so.'

'Oh, I'd like it if he did. Perhaps all *you* need is to be around different people, so that verve rubs off. We both do. Had you thought about events management, though? The kind of person who makes everything run smoothly but isn't centre stage?'

'Not doing weddings.'

'I could shake you sometimes. No, not weddings. All hissy fits and people getting drunk and treading on the bride's train.'

'Have you been to weddings like that?' said Ash, with sudden interest.

'I wish. They'd have been more fun. Nope, I've just got a vivid imagination. I was thinking more about art galleries. Not just private views but travelling exhibitions – where you'd need to get the detail just right. New angles on fundraising.'

'I've never worked on contracts like that.'

'Ash, will you *stop* finding reasons not to do things! You're here, aren't you? In Venice? You're interested in art. What if we checked out some of the small contemporary galleries here to see how they do things? Then let's have a look at revamping your CV. Perhaps you'll trust me to do a good headshot of you on a little canal bridge. You could go back and talk about how Venice has inspired you in a new direction.'

Ash sat quietly for a moment. She felt as though the golden screen of icons had descended and wrapped its glittering eastern richness around her.

'If I was here, you know, I'd do it,' she said quietly. 'I think I could do anything in a place like this. What I'm afraid of is going back and slipping back into the same rut.'

'Do it as though you're doing it for Venice. Target the people who might even bring you back here, all expenses paid.'

'Gianni's hotel?' Ash pulled a rueful face.

'Why not Gianni's hotel? Not because of Gianni. Because

of Davide. He'd know how to cater arts events or would know the people who could.'

'*Carpe diem.*'

'Exactly.'

'What if we go back to the hotel for a bit? I'd like to do a bit of Duolingo. I know it's a bit lame, but it'd be a start. I'll sign up for a class when we're back home.'

'While you're doing that, I'll make a list of galleries. Everything will close at twelve thirty so we can get a quick bite to eat and go window-shopping. That way we won't have people coming up to us trying to sell us things that won't fit in our baggage and that we couldn't afford anyway. We can go back as mystery shoppers to the places we like the look of. What? What is it, Ash?'

'Oh, I don't know. I'm not sure I've got the confidence...'

'Ash, not *that* again. All right, I know what we're going to do first. You'll be doing me a favour too.'

'Oh?'

'We're going to fake it until we make it, as they say. I've been looking up some of the vintage stores in Venice. I've a feeling they're going to be pretty classy – not a 50p rummage bin. I'd like to see how it's done. I'm going to be your personal shopper, Ash.'

Ash brightened.

'Only the first thing we need is a good hairdresser.'

'How will we know who is good? We can't ask the lady

who runs the hotel. She's really nice but her hair looks like a bird's nest.'

'We're going to ask Donatella.'

'But she doesn't like us!'

'She's a bit wary, I'll admit. But she likes herself, Ash. She's not going to recommend anyone who's terrible. That would reflect badly on her. Seriously, asking her is flattering her. Everyone likes flattery. I think even you do though you try not to.'

Chapter Thirteen

20th April – Being New and Jolly by the Rialto

Ash turned to Jules, sitting alongside, and smiled. 'You were right,' she mouthed. Donatella had risen to the occasion and had got simultaneous appointments with what she said were the two most talented stylists at 'New Jolly Style' just around the corner from the Rialto Bridge. Her whole demeanour had changed. The two English girls needed advice from an expert, after all. As Davide told Juliet later, Donatella had at first thought them a bit stand-offish and he'd had to tell her that they were only shy, 'though I'm glad you aren't shy with me, Juliet,' he'd added gallantly. Ash thought 'shy' was the last word she'd use to describe Juliet.

The name of the place had made Ash raise her eyebrows, but as Jules said, 'we want to be new and jolly, don't we? Let's go for it.' It was a large salon, occupying the space of what must have once been two or three shops or a decent-sized trattoria, and it was buzzing with life. Ash liked the clean lines of the place: ivory, red and beige with sparkling chrome fittings, and just the occasional plant in a slender vase to provide a splash of green. It was obvious from the conversations going on around her, even with her limited Italian, that patrons came and came back. Donatella was fussing in the background like a mother hen. Ash had enjoyed even getting her hair washed, by a smiling girl with gentle but firm fingers. The products she used had the tang of the sea, and whatever that miracle conditioner was, the brush had gone through without a tug. She started to relax.

There was an involved conversation she followed in the mirror between Donatella and the stylist of which the only word she could be sure of was 'Facebook.' *I must have misheard.* For a moment it felt a bit like being in a hospital bed listening to two doctors discussing her case, using terminology that meant nothing to her, but that impression was quickly dispelled when Donatella leaned forward and explained what the stylist was proposing.

'Nicoletta thinks you have the face of a *fata,* you know, a fairy, a little elf, only you've been disguising yourself. She wants to bring that out.'

'Oh, not a pixie cut!' cried Ash.

Donatella looked momentarily puzzled, until Nicoletta intervened with another stream of incomprehensible Italian.

'*No, no!* Nothing so drastic. She's going to cut soft layers to enhance the shape of your face. Just a little bit off,' she said, indicating with a finger from where neck met shoulder to just below Ash's chin. 'Easy to care for, but really *chic.*

What the French call *gamine.*'

Ash took a deep breath. 'I trust you.'

'*Brava!*'

'Only what was that about Facebook?'

'Ah yes. They'll keep your face out of it if you prefer, but they would like to film just a little bit. Before, and then speeded up to after. You'd be half a minute on Facebook. They tell me it really helps them get new clients.'

That has to be a good sign. They won't want to make a mess of me then.

'Why not? It's a bit more original than posting selfies. You going for it too, Juliet?'

'As the future proprietor of Lucia Upcycles it's compulsory. But names and faces, please! No publicity is bad publicity.'

Later that morning they were ushered out of the salon with kisses and waves, promising to come back again 'next year.' Donatella, flushed with success, had left for work half an hour earlier. Juliet's long dark hair had been styled into soft waves that framed her face, and as Ash thought, accentuated its oval shape and somehow made her eyes look more lustrous.

'You can see you've Italian blood now.'

Juliet swelled with satisfaction, turning her head from side to side in her reflection in the nearest window. That turned out to be a busy bookshop. A student looked up and smiled at her.

'You see,' said Ash, 'it's having an effect already.'

'And you look gorgeous, Ash. Sort of pert, perky. Pretty and fun.'

Ash preened herself in a neighbouring window, making sure she didn't have an audience first. It was an estate agents, so her soft waves were reflected against descriptions of loft apartments in Castello and Cannaregio. *Cheaper than London, but how could I live in Venice?* Here too the stylist's work had accentuated the delicate lines of her face and made her eyes look bigger, and somehow wistful. *Or perhaps that's because I* am *wistful.*

'Something's not right, though,' she said, frowning.

'Oh?'

'Our clothes. Our shoes.'

'Bingo. What I was thinking too. Only we haven't the money for Luisa Spagnoli,' said Jules.

'Or Gucci.'

'Which is too obvious, anyway. So here's the cunning plan... Holy Mary Mother of God, first.'

'What?'

'Campo Santa Maria Mater Domini, Ash – the square of Holy Mary Mother of God – that's where we are going next. Other side of the Rialto Bridge. There's a big vintage store there.'

The double-fronted shop on Campo Santa Maria Mater Domini was a riot of colour and buzzing with customers. The clothes on sale were designer pieces, but also, the friendly proprietor explained in American-accented English, the work of local seamstresses from the 1950s and 1960s, when a girl would be taken by her mother to her own dressmaker for her trousseau. The young woman was delighted when Juliet explained she'd been thinking about a similar venture in London. 'Here,' she said, thrusting a fistful of flyers into Juliet's hands. 'Put these out for us in your new shop and we'll do the same for you.'

Ash handled the clothes with a kind of sweet sadness. They were so well made and had been so lovingly cared-for. She wondered what it was that had brought these treasured things to where they were. As if the proprietor could read her thoughts, she said, 'We really took off after Covid. People understood that the spread of the virus was helped by pollution, and fast fashion is one of the greatest polluters of all. They also had time in lockdown to clear out their closets – and that, added to a greater sense of community, even here where so many people blow in only as second homeowners, meant that they were happy their clothes were going to someone who would let them live again. Oh, why don't you try that one? *You* could really help *this* live again.' The proprietor picked out a simply but beautifully cut ivory dress with lace trim and no maker's label. 'This is probably Burano lace.'

Ash took the dress and disappeared behind a curtain into a changing booth. What she hadn't bargained for was that in Italy trying on a dress could be a bit of a spectator sport as a moment minute later, the owner bustled in and helped her with the zip and the hooks and eyes, tweaking and stroking the cloth.

'*Bellissima,*' she said.

Ash turned to look at herself in the mirror and gasped. It was one of those garments that really did look better on the person – the right person – than on the hanger. A square neck emphasised the delicacy of her collar bone, the creaminess of her skin. While she guessed it was a dress from the sixties it had the slight drop waist of forty years earlier. The effect, when she moved, was to make her look even more slender.

'Where's my friend?' she said eventually.

'In here!' came a muffled voice. Juliet put her head out from the adjoining booth. 'Ready for this?' she said, her eyes dancing. Juliet stepped out, in vibrant red embroidered Indian silk, in a seventies style dress with bell sleeves that really set off her dark hair and brown eyes.

'Look at *you!*' she exclaimed. 'That dress was waiting for you.'

'Jules, you look stunning,' said Ash.

'We're taking both, aren't we? All we need now are shoes.'

There weren't any that, as Jules said, 'worked' with their dresses and the owner, to her credit, agreed with them and didn't attempt to persuade them into anything that wasn't quite right. She folded their dresses carefully into tissue paper and parcelled them up, assuring them that they didn't need to be washed or drycleaned, as all her merchandise was cleaned before being put out for sale.

The remainder of the vintage tour didn't produce shoes in the right style or size either, although in a shop near Piazza San Marco Ash did find a cream Ferragamo bag that was about the same date as her dress. It had had some repairs done which made it a little cheaper. 'Like it's been through the wars,' Ash said, hugging the bag, 'a bit like myself.' Even though they hadn't been completely successful in their search, Jules was buzzing with what she'd seen of shop layouts and window-dressing. Ash could see from the look on her face that she had already fitted out her shop in her mind's eye, even before she'd found it. There was enough determination in her expression that Ash knew that 'Lucia' was going to happen.

After a bowl of pasta each, somewhere off the Salizzada San Lio – *spaghetti carbonara* for Ash and *penne arrabbiate* for Jules, a meal extended by Pinot Grigio, lots of sparkling water and double espressos – the girls decided that only new shoes would do. 'But we'll choose well, so they last,' said Jules. In one shop in the Strada Nova they found exactly what they were looking for, although, as Jules put it, 'I didn't know it was those shoes until I saw them.' Hers were a dark red, supple leather that matched her dress perfectly and had a vaguely Eastern, hippy vibe. Ash found a pair of cream glacé Mary Janes with a twenties style heel. They went back to the hotel flushed and happy, to hang their dresses on the outside of the wardrobe and to put the handbag and the shoes on a chair as though they were on display.

'Ah!' exclaimed Juliet. 'There's a reason why they call it retail therapy. Only somehow it works better here than on Oxford Street. What say you to going to Davide's this evening all dolled up?' said Juliet.

'Yes. The perfect end to a perfect day,' said Ash, meaning it. She surprised herself by adding, 'I hope Donatella's there. I'd like her to see we've done her proud.'

Donatella was impressed, but not quite in the way Ash and Jules had wanted her to be. The snag was that the two men were impressed too.

'Three girls to two boys was never going to be the right dynamic,' said Jules, as they walked back home. 'But you did a great job diverting Donatella onto the wedding plans.'

'It took up the airtime, anyway,' said Ash, feeling the evening had been a disappointment, after their triumphant walk to the Campo, feeling like a million dollars.

'Gianni's face was a picture,' said Jules. 'Talk about buyer's remorse.'

'I didn't see, really. I mean, I was aware of him out of the corner of my eye, the way you do when someone's looking at you.'

'Unless it's on a webcam. You done good, girl. You didn't

break eye contact with Donatella the whole time. Made her feel the centre of attention, which is just what she wanted. We'll get our invites, you'll see. You ought to be guest of honour, seeing as this mightn't have happened if it hadn't been for you.'

'I don't think that'll get mentioned in the speeches, somehow.'

'That's not what the sad voice is about, though, is it?'

Can't hide anything from her, thought Ash. *She knows me too well.*

'It'll be a for a plus one, won't it, the invite?'

'I don't know,' said Jules. 'I don't know what they do here. But judging by the amount of detail Donatella went into over dinner, you can be pretty sure the seating plan will include someone sleek and unattached either side of you. The way to stop Donatella being jealous is to make her proud of having you to show off.'

'*Me?*'

'Why not you? Look at you. You look fabulous. Ethereal, slender, elegant. By the time you come back here – we come back here – you'll be working for an art gallery and I'll have my own atelier. She was talking about early October, right? She'll want to introduce you to everyone as her new London friend.'

'Beats being the sad sack that was stalking her boyfriend on a webcam.'

'Not a sad sack! None of this would have happened if

you hadn't. We'd have gone to a different restaurant every evening and the most we'd have managed was a mini-flirt with a nice waiter each time. Instead we're regulars.'

'And Davide? More than a mini-flirt?'

Jules paused. 'Omigod I hope so. I really like him. I hope I don't fuck it up like I usually do.'

'How could you? *He* really likes *you*.'

The two girls veered sideways to let past a middle-aged couple, unquestionably English, judging by the woman's Liberty scarf and haughty expression and her husband's linen suit with the silk handkerchief in the breast pocket.

'By fucking him too soon, of course.'

'Well, *really*,' they heard the woman say to her husband, deliberately loudly. 'The people they let into Venice these days.'

The two girls collapsed into laughter. *The best response,* thought Ash. *Much better than calling her a stuck-up cow and giving her the satisfaction of knowing that she's bugged you.*

Chapter Fourteen

The logistics of love-making in a gondola

'There's a WhatsApp from Nirmala,' said Ash later, lying in bed scrolling through her messages. 'She's suggesting another meet-up.' Jules slipped off her dressing gown and got into the bed alongside wearing her 'What are you looking at?' outsize t-shirt that never failed to make Ash smile.

'Let's see if I've got one too,' she said, picking up her phone from the bedside cabinet. 'Yup. Let's see who else is on it. Cora, bless her. Says she's got a six-month contract – oh, it's to make a lot of people redundant. A couple of the IT types. They've put photos up. Ah, they aren't clones of each other after all. And Joe Mannion is there too. He doesn't post often. Bloody hell, Ash, look at his picture!'

Ash scrolled. 'He's in a garden. A really pretty one. I wish I'd a pergola like that.'

'I wish I had a garden to put it in. Blow up the photo.'

Ash's fingers spread across the screen. 'It could be in Italy,' she said, peering at the church dome in the background.

'Pity I'm not art-hysterical,' said Jules. 'I'd've been able to tell where that was.'

'It looks a bit like here, only where would they have a garden like that one in Venice?' She remembered the man she'd glimpsed in Campo Santa Margherita a few days earlier. *Could it have been him?* But what most got her attention in the photo was Joe's expression. *He's smiling the way he did on Hampstead Heath. The way he never did in the three years I was in Gulliver and Brant.* 'No reason why he couldn't have gone to Italy for a holiday,' she said aloud. 'I mean, remember that painting he was sitting in front of on Zoom? That was sort of Italian, wasn't it?'

'I didn't look properly. Wasn't it just a Zoom backdrop, like having the Taj Mahal or Blackpool Winter Gardens? Why don't you write to him?'

'To Joe Mannion? Wouldn't that be a bit weird? I've only ever said three words to him. He's hardly going to be my plus one, is he?'

'I expect you're right. Let's see who else is on here.'

An hour later, Ash turned in her bed, disturbed by the click of a door. Half-asleep, she saw Juliet outlined for a second in the sliver of light from the ensuite, before it went out. But in the phosphorescent glow of her friend's cellphone, Ash glimpsed Juliet's secretive smile.

Her and Davide. I need to give them space.

At breakfast, Ash said, 'I was thinking of skipping dinner tonight.'

'Oh! Why? It's Davide's night off. He was going to treat us to another restaurant he knows. A place where journalists and artists go. He says if I'm serious about my new direction it's the kind of place I should be seen in. You as well.'

'Jules, you and him have the chance of being A Thing. And your ideas are also much further forward. I wouldn't have anything to talk about to anybody I met in a cool sort of restaurant. Not yet. You can case the joint or whatever it's called for me. But most of all spend the time with him.'

Ash saw Juliet swallow and saw that her normally upbeat friend was on the brink of tears.

'Jules?'

'You're the best ever. I promise you I won't fuck up.'

Over Juliet's shoulder Ash saw the man of the German couple at the next table raise his eyebrows at his wife and marvelled at how that Anglo-Saxon word was truly international.

'But what'll you do instead?' asked Jules.

'I'll get some fruit and call it my detox night. I'm going to work on my CV. Upload it to a few job sites.'

'You could do that at home – but I did wonder why you'd brought your PC with you.'

'I could. But it's *carpe diem* again. I feel more confident here, like I've left all sorts of crap behind. Ed. Gullible and Burnt. And all the other same old same old. I know this sounds mad, but I can't help feeling that something of Venice, something of the way I feel different here, will get into my applications if I do them from here.'

Juliet took a swig of her cappuccino. 'All right, on one condition. I get to take a great photo of you today and you put it on your CV. In that cream dress.'

'Deal.'

'That's the best photo anyone's ever taken of me,' said Ash, staring down at Juliet's phone. In the image she was standing on a little brick bridge with one hand on the Istrian stone parapet. Behind her was the rear wall of the tiny church of the Miracoli, faced with veined white marble panels framed by violet-grey strips of a different stone Ash thought she ought to know the name of.

'You've got such a good eye for a composition,' she added. 'And you've made me look happy.'

'Well, aren't you?'

'Here, yes.'

Jules hugged her.

'Not bad, is it, though I say it myself. But you're a natural. I'll be wanting you as a model when I get Lucia up and running.'

'A model? A short-arse like me?'

'Yes – because you're graceful. It's like what I said about you standing like a ballet dancer. They're never tall, are they? But you're real too, not a pale spring onion with saltcellar collar bones.'

'I'm sticking to tonight's detox all the same.'

'You don't have to.'

'I want to. And I want you to have the night of your life.'

Ash sent a silent thanks to Cora from HR for insisting on making sure everyone at Gulliver and Brant did an online course in writing a CV, as part of the redundancy preparation, as it meant she had a sound template. She started by cropping the photo Juliet had taken and pasting it into the space in the top left-hand corner. It meant the Mary-Janes and the vintage handbag weren't visible, but the background of the head and shoulders shot was still recognisably Venice for anyone who knew the place.

Now all I have to do is make myself sound exciting, she thought. *The boring bits are all in place. I just need what Cora called my 'unique selling point.' Stalking men with dogs? Your man won't propose? Call Ashley. No job too small.*

Under hobbies, she added, for the first time in her life, 'studying Renaissance art' and 'learning Italian,' but she wrestled with the profile statement.

'Experienced administrator used to working with creatives.'

Nope. Sounds like I'm a sort of lion-tamer. Only a dull one. What would Juliet put?

An hour later Ashley switched off, feeling she'd achieved

something. 'Art is your mission. Need a reliable someone to take care of marketing, finance and events management, leaving you free to be creative? Look no further.' Four sites now had her profile. *I'd better live up to it.*

She showered, to be out of the way when Juliet came in. *If* Juliet came in.

'Omigod! I've had the time of my life!'

Lying in bed, Ash looked up from the vintage guidebook she'd found in the Acqua Alta second-hand bookstore.

'What on earth are you wearing? What happened to your dress?'

Juliet looked down at her black blouse and skirt, contrasting incongruously with her new red shoes.

'We never did get to the Corte Sconta. We met at Santa Maria Formosa but two waiters had called in sick, so Davide really had to work.'

'And you too, by the looks of things.'

'Yup! I am so *sweaty*. But Davide said I was a natural, even if I could only really deal with the English speakers. He said we make a great team. I got so carried away with it that I said I wanted to wait tables at the wedding.'

'You don't really mean that.'

'Of course not – and he wouldn't hear of it. What I'd like is for him afterwards to lower me into a gondola at the landing stage at the back – one with a *felze*—'

'A what?'

'They really just use them when they're filming costume dramas. They're like little cabins that fit over a gondola for a bit of privacy. Only nowadays everybody wants to be seen and to take photos.'

'Whereas you and him would be making mad passionate love going down the Grand Canal.'

'Well, yes, that would be the idea. Like something out of Casanova.' Juliet pirouetted. 'Oh dear, feel a bit dizzy. Perhaps the gondola wouldn't be such a good idea. I might get seasick. And the gondolier would probably have to sing really loudly to drown out my puking and there'd be complaints.'

Chapter Fifteen

Campo Santa Maria Formosa
26th April

Ash and Jules were sitting at what had become their usual table at Davide's restaurant, eating tiramisu as the square gradually quietened for the afternoon. That is, Ash was cleaning her plate but Juliet was uncharacteristically picking at hers.

'Out with it, Jules. You've been in a funny mood all through lunch.'

'Yup, you caught me. I feel like a louse, Ash, but would you be all right on your own this afternoon?'

'I thought you'd never ask. Of course I would. This afternoon, and tonight.'

Jules got up and came round the table to hug her friend. 'It's just, you know, with us going home on Thursday.'

'Jules, it's fine. I'm happy for you. Really I am.'

The slight awkwardness that had hung over the lunch, despite the beautiful day, disappeared. Davide came up then wearing a shy smile Ash could sense even though as a waiter half his face had to be covered, and unannounced put a Cynar in front of her. Without a word he put a tall glass of a dark pink fruit juice before Jules and touched her wrist fleetingly.

'What's that?' asked Ash.

'Um. That's pomegranate.'

'And?'

'It's supposed to be good for sex drive.' Jules looked uncharacteristically awkward.

Ash glanced round, to check nobody was in earshot. 'You need it?'

'Well, if it doesn't work, it's still a detox. I'm a bit nervous, if I'm honest. If we were at home I'd want us to wait longer. I'd want him to be "the one"' she said, apostrophising with her finger-tips. 'But Stansted beckons.'

'Go for it.'

'You're a mate.'

'You'd do the same for me – that's if I gave you half the chance.'

Ash waited, expecting reassuring words from her loyal friend, but instead Jules didn't seem to be listening. She had her hand around the glass of juice but was staring into the distance.

'Jules?'

'Over there. Look. Does he look familiar to you?'

Ash twisted round in her chair. There was a man with a

sketchpad leaning against the wall of the church. She could see the movement of his head as he glanced up at the square and back at his drawing. *That's your life, is it? Looking at men from a distance?* Aloud, she said, 'He looks like Joe Mannion. Like that man I saw when we were having coffee that time.'

'Well, I read somewhere that everybody has something like six doubles somewhere in the world,' said Juliet.

Ash remembered Joe making his way over to her at that work do and how she'd got up and started dancing rather than talk to him. Then there was that time on Hampstead Heath when he'd been about to tell her something only Wanda had come up and sunk her manicure into his arm. She felt mean. *Poor Joe, what harm was there in him? And he really stood up to Rupert Brant that time.*

'Mind if I take a closer look?' she said.

'Be my guest.'

'Won't be a minute. He'll probably look nothing like him close up.'

But as she got closer, the resemblance got stronger. Ash hesitated, hung back, for the man who looked like Joe was intent on his drawing. Then he looked up at his subject and registered the presence of the girl a few feet away, where there hadn't been anyone before. His eyes widened.

'Ashley!'

'What are *you* doing here?'

Joe gestured with the sketchbook. 'Living,' he said.

'Can I see?'

He held out the drawing. Ash prepared herself to say something polite and then saw there was no need. Looking at the delicacy of the pencil sketch of the square, the hotel with its fluttering pennants, the cluster of tables outside Davide's restaurant, she said, 'You've got it,' with genuine admiration. 'I never knew.'

'Thank you.'

Then she remembered. 'That mural. The one we could see on Zoom.'

'I did that. Couldn't resist the temptation of a blank wall.'

'I'd no idea you were an artist.'

'I'm not really. I'm more of a draughtsman. A copyist, I suppose. I didn't invent the mural. I squared up the design from a painting in a book, making sure everything lined up and was accurate to the original. I was an accountant, after all.'

'Was?'

'I still do a bit. As a contractor. Just to keep my hand in and my professional standing up to date.'

There was a short silence, then Ash said, 'Well, *I* think you've got talent.'

'Thank you. Only I think I might be better at saving other people's art.'

'What do you mean? Donating to Venice in Peril?'

'Not exactly. I've enrolled at UIA – *Università Internazionale dell'Arte,'* said Joe. His Italian accent was so convincing that Ash was startled. Even his face and manner when he spoke the language looked different.

'I'm training to be an art restorer – or conservator, to be exact. I get the *vaporetto* across to Le Zitelle on the Giudecca every morning to go to Villa Hériot. I don't know how long you're going to be here for, but I'd love to take you round.'

Ash remembered to stop gaping. *Not a good look.*

'Is that where that garden is? The one you put on WhatsApp?'

'You saw it?' He looked pleased. 'It's not the villa's garden, no, but it's close by, on the Giudecca.'

Ash found herself wanting to know who took it, hoping it was a selfie. All she said was, 'We're going back on Thursday.'

'We?'

'Juliet and me. You remember her? She's sitting outside that restaurant over there.'

'I remember. She posted on WhatsApp that you were here.'

'And you didn't get in touch?' said Ash reproachfully.

'Well, I was going to, only...' Ash saw he was flushing. 'That is, you mightn't have wanted to see me. I mean, if you'd been looking forward to being here as much as I was, the last person you might've wanted to run into was Joe from Accounts.'

'Not true,' said Ash, realising she wasn't just being polite.

'I should have realised that was you two sitting over there. I was so busy trying to get the perspective right that I hadn't looked properly at the people.'

'Come over. She'd love to see you again.'

Joe closed up the sketchpad and put it into a bag. Ash wondered then how many people got to see his work; it was evident that he wasn't intending to show it off to Juliet or Gianni. They walked back across the square.

'Oh, Gianni's turned up,' said Ash.

'Gianni?'

'Oh… um… it's a bit complicated to explain. Gianni's just a friend, only he's a bit boring sometimes. He works in that hotel over there.'

'You're staying *there?*'

'Ah, no… a place near the station. Perhaps you won't think he's boring, poor lad.'

'Why do you hang around with this Gianni, then? I can't imagine you or Juliet having boring friends.'

'I suppose he was a sort of penpal,' said Ash, casting around for something that had enough resemblance to the truth to put Joe off the scent.

'You mean you met him on a dating app?'

'No – nothing like that. I'll tell you later.'

Joe frowned. 'He's not stalking you, is he?'

This was so unnervingly close to what Ash had thought about herself that her 'No!' came out more loudly than she had intended.

'I'll shut up, shall I?' muttered Joe. They were approaching the table. Juliet got up and hugged Joe, something that had never happened when they'd been at work – even when it had been allowed. Ash wished she'd been as spontaneous.

'Fancy meeting you here? Gianni – Joe. And this is Killer.' Juliet made the introductions. 'Gianni speaks good English. I've never heard Killer say anything.'

'*Nessun problema,*' said Joe. '*Ormai parlo un po' d'italiano.*'

'Impressive!' said Juliet. 'Where did you learn that?'

'I only said I spoke a bit of Italian. It was one of my long-range plans.'

Ash decided to say nothing of her five minutes a day Duolingo. She had done loads of the online drills but found it hard to get up the courage to speak when faced with a real live Italian, and in Venice as she had expected, just about everybody spoke English. Joe and Gianni were now in an animated conversation she could only follow bits of and that only because they seemed to be talking about some software or other, so their words were peppered with English. She exchanged glances with Juliet. That was the difference that really knowing a language inside out made. It was the first time she'd seen Gianni look remotely lively. There was a five second pause in the conversation and Ash jumped in.

'Anyone would think you'd been living here for ages, Joe.'

'Not ages,' he said, smiling. 'But the best part of six months. I'm in my first year of my course but I came early so I could get acclimatised and to find a flat I was happy with. I forced myself not to socialise with English speakers. I meant to tell you – that time we were on Hampstead Heath. Only we were interrupted.'

'But how do you get to stay here with Brexit and everything? Did they give you a student visa? We had to get our passports stamped,' said Ash.

'Sorry to interrupt – just going to the bog,' said Juliet.

'Oh – right, no problem,' said Ash.

'I need to take Killer to do *pipì*,' said Gianni.

Joe turned back to Ash. 'My full name is Joseph Ignatius Mannion. Only don't put that on social media, will you? My old ones are from Galway and Limerick – he came over to work on building sites and Ma was a nurse. I was brought up in Cricklewood but I've been registered since birth as an Irish citizen.'

'Before it became fashionable, then,' said Juliet. 'Lucky you.'

'I *am* lucky,' he said, suddenly serious. 'Both my parents were desperate for me to get a job in an office. A job, my Da said, where I wouldn't need to bother my head about the weather. I knew they'd made sacrifices for me so I went along with accountancy training. It wasn't art college but I wasn't going to let go of my dream so I did things part-time – evening courses I never told anyone about. It kept me sane through the accountancy exams even if it did mean I had some repeats. Then Covid came and I realised that the only life I have is the one I've got now. After that I had another stroke of luck. Do you believe in signs, Ash?'

Ashley couldn't answer for a moment. She was still processing the longest speech she had ever heard Joe Mannion make.

'What, star signs, or more like destiny trying to tell you something?' she said eventually.

'Destiny trying to tell you something. I know that doesn't make any sense coming from an accountant.'

'Maybe.' *Yes, probably. Like you being the last person I expected to meet in Venice.* 'So what was your revelation?'

'There was also a bit of land in Ireland, farmed near Limerick by a bachelor uncle. He got Covid at a farmers' mart, and because he was a lifetime smoker it did for him. It turned out he'd left the farm to me. There was a letter along with his will, urging me to sell it as it was "a misfortunate, shitehole kip of a place. Only an eejit would earn his living that way."'

Ash's eyes widened. Joe's voice had changed completely, just as when he spoke Italian. It wasn't just accent; Joe's voice had been someone else's – that tobacco-stained Irish farmer's. She wanted to ask him if he'd ever considered acting but realised there were lots of questions she wanted to ask him. *Joe's been a colleague for three years but never really* known *him.*'

'But it wasn't misfortunate after all?'

'Not a bit of it. Turned out the Irish Development Agency were after those few acres, to expand an industrial park, and there was a compulsory purchase order on it in any case. My solicitor told me to put up a bit of a fight, about how it had been in the family generations and all that. I did what he told me, and their offer went up. Flanagan wanted me to keep fighting as they were desperate for the site and might stump up more cash, but I was more than happy with what I was getting and he was probably only after a bigger fee. I sold my uncle's herd to a neighbour.'

'So you're a rich man,' said Ash quietly. She found this news made her feel uneasy.

'Not from the cows, no, from the IDA. But I'm comfortable. I don't need to worry about things. I *am* a bit of a worrier, or I would have gone to Art School back when I was younger no matter what anyone said. But it's enabled me to make this change. I'm thirty-two. Most of the people on the course are in their early twenties, new graduates. It's not art school, either. I know I can earn money with what they'll train me to do and do it here. Seventy-five per cent of Europe's art treasures are in Italy, Ash, and they all need looking after. And I'll still be able to paint in my spare time and to talk about it if I want. It's a normal hobby for an art conservator, after all. My flat is the top floor of a building in Cannaregio. They'd call it a penthouse if it was a London agent selling it but it's a bit more basic than that. I love sitting up there with my coffee in the morning. I'm thinking I'll paint a series of pictures of the chimney pots and belltowers.'

'Like Carpaccio,' said Ash.

'You've seen that?' said Joe, smiling. 'The one where they're rescuing the relic from the Grand Canal?'

'I'd like one of your paintings,' Ash heard herself say.

Joe's smile got wider.

'You're the first person who's said that to me. My flat belonged to an artist so for wet or cold days there's a studio space, glass panels instead of roof-tiles so lots of light. Would you have time to come and see it before you go?'

'I'd love to, only I don't know if there'll be time.' She felt a stab of guilt. *I want to go there without Juliet. At least the first time.* She felt herself flushing. *What makes you think there's going to be a second time?*

'What's the matter?' said Joe. 'Did I say something wrong?'

'No – not at all. I was just thinking. I've known you for ages, Joe, but didn't know this side of you at all.'

'It's not a side, Ash. This is who I always was. Only everyone thought I was "Ken Dull, the most interesting man in Dorking," didn't they? I am sure you did.'

'Ken Dull? You're a Python fan?'

'Yes, but I don't like shouting and I can't give a cat influenza.'

Ash laughed. To her surprise she realised she was tearing up.

'I've even booked a visit to Scotland – a *Monty Python and the Holy Grail* tour to Doune Castle and to Eilean Donan.'

'You'll probably be sharing them with *Game of Thrones* fans these days.'

'I am a bit old-fashioned, aren't I?'

'Vintage, perhaps. Which never goes out of fashion. Which reminds me – Juliet's got plans. Upcycling clothes. Where's she got to? Oh – over there. Juliet and Davide – the waiter she's talking to – they're a Thing.'

Seeing Ash wave, Juliet came back, and with some prompting, told Joe about the conversation at the Rialto which had set her off on her new direction. And as if by a signal, Gianni and Killer returned too.

'Have you got those sketches with you, Jules?' asked Ash.

'I've left them in the hotel,' said Juliet, but Ash could see this was a fib and that her friend was just shy of showing them to Joe, as the sketchbook from the stationer's in Calle San Cassiano had gone with them everywhere. 'It's just an idea,' Juliet went on. 'I've not acted on it yet. Not like you, Joe.'

'Do it,' said Joe, decisively. 'I'll help you out with the accounting. Your VAT returns and all that. *Pro bono*, mind.

I'm sure Gianni here would give you a hand with your website too.'

Gianni nodded with such enthusiasm that Ash thought his head would roll off. There was something about Joe, this new Joe, that she could see others found irresistible.

At that moment Davide appeared at Joe's elbow.

'*Desidera qualcosa, signore?*'

'*Un amaro, grazie.*'

Davide was about to go and get the order, when Juliet stopped him. 'Davide, you've not met Joe. He was our colleague in London. We've just run into him by accident. Wasn't that a coincidence?'

'A real coincidence,' said Davide.

Ash frowned. Something was off in the way Davide spoke, but she couldn't put her finger on it.

'*Piacere*, Joe,' said Davide, extending his hand. Joe shook, and Ash shook off the doubt.

'*Torno subito,*' said Davide, and went off.

Joe turned back to Juliet. 'It's a good business model you have. And this is absolutely the moment. Things are getting tough back there and they'll get tougher. You forget that in a place like Venice, where apart from when there was Covid, there have always been tourists. Shortages in the supply chain, shortages in people's pockets. And we're maybe realising now that we just can't go on draining lakes in Uzbekistan or wherever to make even more novelty t-shirts. You might want to think about some pop-ups, just to get yourself on the map, even if you're going to be running the business from home. Some London boroughs have incentives in place as they're worrying about their emptying high streets.'

'You're really well-informed, Joe.'

For the first time since he'd sat down, Joe hesitated. 'I've a confession to make.'

'Go on,' said Ash.

'Well, when we had all those Zoom meetings, with your man banging on about sunlit uplands and the new post-Covid dawn and all that crap, when the only sunlit uplands he was thinking about were in some tax haven or other... well, I had an old computer set up alongside the work one and once he was off on his flights of fancy – his fibs I mean – I was reading articles to stop myself going insane with boredom. That's when I wasn't looking at webcams of Venice, of course.'

Ash's coffee cup clattered in its saucer. She couldn't look at Juliet directly but could see out of the corner of her eye that Juliet was also doing her best not to look at her.

'Oh, which ones? Have you been spying on that seagull at the Rialto too?' said Ash.

'You were doing the same thing as me?' said Joe, delighted. 'All roads lead to Venice, then, only you've to leave your car at Piazzale Roma and walk.'

'Ash,' said Juliet, leaning forward. 'Seeing as Davide has asked would I go to the Lido with him this afternoon, what's to stop you going to see Joe's flat, or his college? As long as Joe is free.'

'I'm free,' said Joe, smiling.

Then all three guiltily turned to the by now silent member of the group.

'I have the afternoon off today,' said Gianni. Ash felt her heart sink. 'Only I've got some news too.'

'Tell us, Gianni,' said Joe, seeing him hesitate.

Gianni shrugged. 'It cannot be put off any longer, I think. I am going with Donatella to see the priest. It is our destiny. We will agree the day with him.'

'Congratulations,' said Joe, energetically shaking Gianni's hand. The girls followed his example, but Ash felt, looking at Gianni's expression, that the marriage announcement had put a dampener on the day. Gianni didn't look joyful. He just looked as though he was accepting the inevitable.

'I hope… that is I would like very much, if you were all to come to the wedding. You were there when I proposed after all.'

Ash felt a guilty flush rise up her neck. She exchanged glances with Juliet.

'Try to stop us,' said Juliet. 'A wedding in Venice? What's not to like?'

'Where will it be?' asked Joe.

'Over there,' said Gianni, inclining his head in the direction of Santa Maria Formosa.

'Of course, where else?' said Ash. 'You'll even be on the webcam.'

There was a beat of silence, in which Ash could feel her face heating up even more.

'You've watched my webcam?' said Gianni. Ash thought he looked more pleased about this than he had about his marriage announcement.

'We watched webcams all over Venice,' cut in Juliet. 'Piazza San Marco, the Rialto, various places in the Dorsoduro. But we'll be watching yours more than any of them from now on.'

Ash gazed at her friend in admiration. But Gianni gave no sign he'd noticed any awkwardness. He took off on a long and animated story about how he'd persuaded the hotel to install the webcam though they'd thought guests wouldn't like it. 'Far from the truth. But we do get more demands for rooms facing the square than we used to, so that they can tune in every morning to the view they remember, once they're back in Manhattan or wherever. I've also seen people wave up at it, so you know they've got friends at home watching.'

Ash couldn't help herself. 'Don't you worry about who might be watching *you*? Or who might be watching us at this very moment sitting having our coffee?'

'Not really. It's not as if you can really make people out that clearly. You'd probably recognise Killer before you'd recognise me. And Venice is so much about seeing and being seen. It always has been.'

'Well, I hope there are lots of people watching when you and Donatella in a lovely dress come out of that door over there,' said Joe. 'People all over the world chucking virtual rice over you both.'

'You'll come too, won't you?'

'Me? Oh, I'd be honoured. But you shouldn't feel obliged to invite me.'

'I don't,' said Gianni, 'I'd like you to be there. And if Juliet will be there with Davide you'd be company for Ashley.'

My plus one.

Joe looked at Ash with a shy smile. 'That would be really special,' he said. Ash told herself this meant being invited to the wedding, rather than because he'd be going with her. But she still felt Joe's eyes on her.

Gianni smiled. 'It'll be special for me having my friends there. I think you're the only ones I've got apart from Davide are just mine, if you see what I mean, more than mine and Donatella's.'

Ash wondered if she was going to cry.

'Where will you have the reception?' she asked, though she was pretty sure of the answer.

'In the hotel,' he said. 'But the restaurant – Davide's restaurant – will do the catering. Only Davide himself will have the day off. He's standing up for me.'

'Your best man?' said Joe.

'My best man. My best friend,' said Gianni loyally. 'We'll have our wedding night there too.'

'What about the honeymoon?' asked Ash. She was beginning to wonder if that was going to be no further than Murano.

Gianni laughed, as if he'd read her thoughts. 'Ah no, we'll go away for that. We're undecided between Croatia and a Greek island. Everybody wants to come to Venice for their honeymoon so Venetians have to go somewhere else.'

'Makes sense,' said Ash, thinking about singing gondoliers and Burano lace veils – all the little fantasies she'd had about the unknown man with the dog. Only she wasn't thinking about Gianni and was pretty sure she didn't need either. She realised though that she did want Joe to see her in the dress from Campo Santa Maria Mater Domini.

Chapter Sixteen

The Giudecca
26th April

Ash and Joe walked through a side gate and through a quiet garden up to the steps into the portico of the Villa Hériot. Ash paused, as Joe watched her, to look out across the shimmering water to a couple of islets covered in trees. A few boats were moored to a landing stage. The quiet contrast with the view from the other side of the long strip of the island of the Giudecca was total. She had turned from the vaporetto stop at Le Zitelle to look back at one of the most famous, and surely the most unique cityscape in the world. Her hand still felt the imprint of his as he solicitously reached out for her as they stepped off the bucking vaporetto. She hadn't really needed the help but there was something chivalrous and old-fashioned about the gesture she'd liked. Then they'd walked through wider streets of modest blocks of flats with washing hanging out, past a library and playground and below the high wall of what Joe had explained was a women's prison ('but hardly Ryker's Island').

'It's nice here,' she said, 'but very different from Venice proper.'

'I'd thought about living here. There is a little supermarket on the Giudecca, a chemist, all the things you really need, but it might have been too close to the office, so to speak. And who wouldn't want to commute to work on a vaporetto?'

'Maybe if you'd always had to do it you wouldn't like it.'

'Right enough. But I also didn't want to interfere, in a way. There are some non-Venetians living over here, but not to the extent there are in the main part of Venice. So many people have been edged out to Mestre on the mainland. This is a proper working-class district. That deserves a sort of preservation, in my opinion, as much as somewhere like Versailles.'

Ash was impressed by Joe's sensitivity, his ability to pick up things that others missed. But she also sensed that Joe was nervous.

'I hope you like this place. It means a lot to me – I mean, both Villa Hériot and that you should like it.'

Now, standing on the steps of the villa and looking at the quiet gardens around with their marble benches and a squat little pillar that could almost serve as a table, she said, 'It's beautiful. You are so lucky that you get to come here every day!'

Joe smiled. Ash remembered again that she had never

seen him smile at work; he'd just been a dour accountant in a dark suit and tie. It transformed his face, warmed his dark eyes. For a mad moment she wondered what it would be like to touch his curling hair – hair that before lockdown had been kept rigidly short, as if otherwise it might have wanted to make a break for it. Juliet was right – he *did* look a bit like Aidan Turner – or Byron. *What was it they said about him? Mad, bad and dangerous to know? Joe isn't any of those things. And didn't Byron swim in the Grand Canal? I can't imagine Joe doing that – not even this new Joe.*

'I know I'm lucky,' he said, but she saw a shadow flit across those eyes. 'Shall we go in?'

She listened as Joe explained who the villa had been built for. The style, he told her, with its stilted arches, was that peculiar mix of native Venetian and Moorish influence that had come before Gothic. 'Ruskin hated it, of course,' he said.

Of course. I've vaguely heard of Ruskin. There was that film with Emma Thompson's husband in it, wasn't there? I'd better look him up.

'But this is nineteenth-century pastiche, though done to the highest standards,' Joe went on. He explained to her how it was possible to tell ancient architecture from relatively modern. There was a sharpness about the new, architectural details machine cut rather than carved, a regularity about windows and doorframes. 'When you are a restorer – or better, a conservator – you have to make sure you don't impose on the painting or the sculpture or the building you are working on, your own modern ideas of what it ought to look like. You have to get into the mind and the hands of the artist or craftsman who made it and in most cases use only the materials and tools he would have had.'

They went in the main entrance and Ash gasped at the fine staircase flowing down the brick well of the central part of the villa. Built of creamy Istrian stone, it divided at the first floor, where a woman came out of an office and smiled at Joe before going on upstairs.

'It's very quiet,' whispered Ash.

'They're working. You can almost hear the hum of concentration. On the hour they'll come out and this will look quite different. Let me show you the library in the meantime.'

They went upstairs. In the room next to where art journals and books were shelved behind glass and wood, Ash could hear a voice speaking authoritatively, though she couldn't make out the words. Then there was a scraping of chairs, a gathering up, unmistakable noises wherever you were in the world, Ash thought, of a lesson coming to an end. They were right on cue, for an instant later the bells at the Redentore started up. Ash couldn't tell from where they stood if the notes she heard chasing each other up and down the scale were only from that church or whether the sound was mingled with that of other belfries – San Giorgio, for instance, just a little further along but across a narrow strip of water, or the bells in the commanding campanile of San Marco itself.

'Bells sound different, don't they, when there is water all around,' she started to say, when the doors opened. She remembered thinking, *that's something I could never have said to Ed. He'd have said I was cracked.* Students flowed out of the lecture room, portfolios under their arms. In contrast to the patrician style of the building, they were dressed in simple lab coats with the initials UIA, or in jeans and white t-shirts with the same logo. Some were wearing visors or face masks, though pushed up or down. Following her gaze, Joe said, 'We were already prepared for Covid, in a way. We wear those masks because of the dust or fumes. Here, let's move back into the stairwell.'

Looking up, Ash could see a balustrade running around an upper floor, where heavy wooden doors stood open; she longed to explore. The walls were of plain brick, adorned only by occasional carved roundels, which with the light that came in from the skylight gave the impression that they were in a courtyard open to the sky.

Without thinking, she said, 'You could imagine a bride coming down that staircase, a very special kind of bride. She'd have designed and made her dress herself. Lots of antique lace.'

There was a pause before Joe answered, enough time for her to blush.

'Yes, I could imagine that,' he said.

'It's Gianni's news put the idea into my head,' she babbled. 'Only they'll be getting married in Santa Maria Formosa and crossing the square to the hotel. And I can't quite imagine Donatella in anything upcycled.'

'I barely know Gianni,' said Joe, 'But I don't think he's going to be that happy.'

Ash glanced up at him.

'Have you ever been in love, Ash?' he asked.

'Me? Oh, I don't know… I mean, I suppose so… it's hard to say.'

'*I* have, that is to say, I am, only—' Joe broke off as a petite young woman tugged his sleeve.

Ash felt a jolt of disappointment. She remembered seeing the man she now knew must have been Joe, in Campo Santa Margherita, in that group of students. *Of course he's in love. He's met some beautiful Italian girl here – probably this is her, looking adoringly up at him. That would explain how he speaks the language so well.*

'*Ciao,* Ash,' said the girl, turning to her. 'We've heard so much about you,' she went on in charmingly accented English.

'*Me?*'

'*Certo!* We all love Joe here and want him to be happy. Are you making him happy, Ash?'

'I… well, I don't know. It doesn't really look like it, does it?' To Ash's surprise, Joe had covered his face with his hands. He was murmuring something. The girl tugged playfully at one of his wrists, until he uncovered his face. Ash saw an expression that was an odd mixture of embarrassment and relief.

'You've big feet for someone your size, Chiara,' he said ruefully.

'Well, someone needs to say something if you won't,' Chiara retorted, unabashed. 'Got to go, people,' she added, kissing Ash fleetingly on the cheek before landing an ineffectual little punch on Joe's upper arm and rushing off.

Joe rubbed the back of his hand against his forehead.

'Joe, I think you need to tell me what's going on,' she said quietly.

'I expect you'd like to go back to your hotel, wouldn't you? Then I'd better do what honorable men do in those old films.'

'What's that?'

'Go and find a twelve-bore and make an end of myself.'

'No, I just want you to tell me what everybody else seems to know. Not just these people here. You knew Davide already, didn't you? He speaks perfect English and you were at our table but he spoke to you in Italian. I thought at first it was because you manage to look Italian – because you do, in a way - but he must have heard you speaking English and you were introduced as Joe.'

'That'll be my take-away. That I look Italian, I mean. Better than looking like dull Joe Mannion.'

'Stop it, Joe! You're hardly dull. Nobody who can paint the way you do could be. And stop changing the subject.'

'Sorry. I didn't think Chiara was going to give the game away here, at least. I must have come across more confident of success than I really am. Or something got lost in translation.'

'What game? Success in what?' But remembering her blooper over *fidanzata* Ash felt some sympathy for him.

'Let's finish the tour and then we can talk in the garden. Somewhere where we won't be overheard.'

'All right,' said Ash. *I do want to see up there. But I want to know how much of this is coincidence.* It was quickly obvious that it wasn't just Chiara who adored Joe. Lots of other students greeted him affectionately in the airy studios they walked through or looked up from their easels and smiled. Some didn't look around at all, completely absorbed as they were in painstakingly cleaning an intricate piece of Baroque wood carving – Ash saw one young man working on what looked like a choir stall and wondered how many more of those not very comfortable seats needed his efforts. Another was bringing out the luminous colours on a large canvas of the Madonna and Child, darkened by age and the smoke of countless votive candles. Joe would put his finger to his lips as they passed these students, as if they were praying. But after a while, Ash ceased to be surprised at how many of them knew who she was. She liked the way Joe was oddly protective of her. He would guide her by putting his hand gently on her shoulder, or on her back guiding her into a room. In anyone else she might have resented this. She tried to imagine Gianni doing the same and recoiled at the thought, so much so that Joe looked down at her, momentarily perplexed, until she reassured him with a smile, turning towards him. Ash met a couple of Joe's teachers too.

'We are lucky to have Joe here,' said one. Ash caught sight of the name Cecilia on her lanyard.

'I can already see that he has a great career ahead of him in the art world,' said the woman. 'It is my fervent wish that whatever he does, he will find some time to come back here and teach for us too. But I think you have known our Joe some time, no?'

For a moment Ash didn't know what to say. *I thought I knew him, but now I don't think I did at all.*

'We were colleagues,' she said. 'Joe was very respected and conscientious.' *That was true,* she thought. *But we all thought he was boring. Aren't being respected and conscientious good qualities too?* She glanced at him. 'I think he is much happier here, though.'

Cecilia smiled. 'Sometimes though I threaten him with making him look at our finances. It is not so common, I think, to find someone with his talent as a craftsman who also understands figures, though a Renaissance artist would have had to do precisely that.'

Joe inclined his head. 'I'd be pleased to help, Professor Girotti.'

'We'll leave that to the accountants, dear man.' She turned back to Ash. 'You will be coming to live in Venice, then?'

Ash felt her mouth open like a fish. 'I wish. I have to go back to London on Thursday,' she managed.

'To do what?'

'Oh… I don't know. Look for another job I suppose. Not another temporary contract.'

'Ah yes, *tempo determinato,*' said Professor Girotti. 'So many of our young people have this problem. And your specialism?'

'I'm in Marketing, or I was.'

'But is your heart in it, Ash?'

Ash was about to say 'no,' but as if Juliet was at her shoulder prompting her, she heard herself go off in quite a different direction.

'Not in that kind of Marketing. Helping people to sell cars doesn't really nurture the soul, even if people need them.'

'Except here,' said Professor Girotti.

'Except here, of course. But I think I am good at the administration that lies behind a good marketing campaign. The unseen bit, if you like. Only I would like to take that into a different setting. Arts administration, for instance. Art – contemporary art as well – is having a resurgence post-Covid. People who have saved money during Covid – I've been working on some focus groups that show that quite a few have, while for others, depending on what they did for a living, Covid has been an economic and social disaster – well, they are looking to spend it on something that lasts. Some want to do something that will recall for them a loved one. So, I thought I would approach some of the London galleries and dealerships. Perhaps —' she glanced at Joe and was gratified to see he was listening intently. 'Well, perhaps there might even be opportunities for conservators. I mean,' she plunged on, encouraged by Joe's attention and the interested tilt of Professor Girotti's head, 'just a few months ago they even found that a painting in the Ashmolean Museum in Oxford that everyone had thought was a fake was quite possibly the real thing.'

'I remember,' said Professor Girotti. 'A Rembrandt. Someone matched the wood of the panel with another painting of his. We have a dendrochronologist on the staff here too.'

'Matteo is amazing,' said Joe. 'He can tell by the age and origin of the wood panel it's painted on if an image is likely to be what it appears to be.'

'Do you have a card, Miss Ash?'

'Oh... no I don't.'

'I know where you can get them made,' said Joe.

'I will be able to contact you through *Signor* Mannion in the meantime, *vero*?'

'Er, yes... yes of course.'

'We will stay in touch then,' said Professor Girotti, shaking Ash's hand. '*A presto,* I hope. *Carpe diem.*'

'*Carpe diem,*' echoed Ash, as the professor walked briskly away.

Outside in the April sunshine, Joe said, 'She was impressed by you.'

'Really?'

'So she should be. You were impressive at Gulliver and Brant, too. Only the fools probably never told you so. You sounded so determined there. A woman who knew where she was going.'

Me? Aloud, Ash said, 'the only place I am going now is back to London in a couple of days.'

'I'm sorry you are. Just after finding you again.'

'I couldn't stay on and live in Venice even if I wanted to,' she said.

'Wouldn't you want to, Ash?'

'You only get ninety days at one go now because of Brexit. No more than a hundred and eighty in a year.'

'So come for ninety days then and see how you get on.'

'I couldn't afford that.'

'You could,' he said huskily, then cleared his throat. 'If your London gallery plans don't work out, though there's no reason why they shouldn't, take one of those short-term contracts they advertise on Linkedin you could do distantly.

And, um, you could live in my flat. I'm sure Hetty would like you.'

'Hetty?'

'My cat.'

'Oh!' Ash smiled her relief. 'You really have settled here.'

'I have. Look, Ash... could we... would you come and eat with me? There's a little place down the far end of the island, the Giudechina.'

'I'd love to. But first of all tell me what on earth is going on.'

He put his hands on her upper arms.

'I promise. Only, first of all I want you to forget the Joe Mannion you thought you knew. The kind of man who'd get excited about Excel spreadsheets and forecasts. The one who didn't know how to enjoy himself at staff parties. The one who never had the courage to say what he wanted.'

'Perhaps you weren't really given the chance,' said Ash in a small voice.

'I've never been very good with things that feel like compulsory social events. Or small talk. I kept going by immersing myself in work – because, strangely enough, it *is* satisfying when you can get numbers to tally – because the job gave me what I needed to live. To be able to go home and paint or go to galleries.'

'I wish I'd known you did that. I'd have gone with you.'

'Do things with me now – would you?' He looked to Ash as excited as a little boy at the prospect of a train set.

'Yes.'

'Ash. I've got to tell you something. Well, I think you know, seeing as Chiara let the cat out of the bag. But I've no idea what it means to you.'

'Say it, Joe. *Carpe diem.*'

'I always – how can I put this? I always admired you, Ash.'

'Me?'

'You. I never spoke because – well, partly because I didn't like people knowing my business in that company, though with the students here I find I *want* them to know. And I never thought I'd get anywhere. I knew from the watercooler talk that you were spoken for, even if, to be honest, I thought you didn't look particularly happy.'

'I wasn't.'

'I'm sorry you weren't – only of course I'm not sorry. Are you still…'

'Free? Oh yes.'

His fingers pattered against her arms for emphasis. 'When I saw you here in Venice I thought it was meant, somehow. Well, I mean it was and it wasn't. You and Juliet planning that holiday for ages and me planning a new life here – that was pure coincidence.'

'How did you know Jules and I were going to be here?'

Joe looked shamefaced. 'She told me.'

'*Told* you?'

'We've been in touch since Hampstead Heath.' Looking

at her astonished face, Joe said, 'Don't take on at her, please. She's fiercely protective of you. Only once I'd convinced her I was serious about you, I had to stop her talking me up to you. I wanted to do that myself, you see. Only I was afraid you'd think I was a pure eejit, not saying anything for *years,* hoping that Venice would work its magic instead. But Gianni was in the picture – him and his wee dog.'

'How long has he known?' said Ash, closing her eyes.

'Well, only about ten days, same as Davide.'

Ash opened her eyes. *Thank heavens. He doesn't know about the webcam. Jules, you're a mate. You always have been.*

'Once it was obvious that Davide and Juliet were going to be a thing,' Joe went on. 'she brought him in on the plot. That's how I know him, but I hadn't met Gianni until I was introduced to him when you were there. So it all went on behind your back, I'm afraid.'

'All's fair in love and war,' said Ash in a shaky voice.

'I don't know who it is said that first but it's completely wrong. Love is seldom fair and war never is.'

'Oh Gawd. So you've always known I was going to be in Venice at this time?'

'Yes.'

Ash remembered Juliet's secret smile in the phosphorescent light of the telephone, that night in the hotel. 'And you've been texting, you and her? Regularly?'

'I'm afraid so.'

'So none of this was coincidence?'

'Walking through Campo Santa Margherita that time? Nope. Though it was all I could do to not turn round and look at where I knew you'd be sitting.'

'That was *planned*? Were there other times you were spying on me and I didn't know you were there?'

'A few times, I'll confess.'

'Where?'

'Campo Santa Maria Formosa, of course.'

'I never saw you.' Then it dawned. 'You were watching on the webcam? Gianni's webcam?'

'I was that soldier. And sometimes I was there for real, but you didn't see me.'

Ash started to laugh. 'Did Juliet text you that night after you put up that photo on WhatsApp, that one of you in the garden?'

'Yup. She was urging me to do something. Reminding me that time was running out. So we set up that I'd be sketching in the Campo.'

'And she'd have the afternoon off with Davide...'

'Well, to be honest, I think she wanted that anyway.'

'And here was me worrying I was cramping her style.'

'Then you admired my drawing. That was just the best thing ever, Ash. I could tell you weren't just being polite.'

'I wasn't. I did admire it. I admire you, Joe.'

Ash looked up at Joe, holding his gaze. But just at that moment a shoal of students, as lively as porpoises, burst out of the institute and down the steps. Some called out '*Ciao,* Joe, *bravo* Joe' and other things Ash didn't understand but which made Joe smile sheepishly.

'I suppose we'd better go and eat,' he said.

'Not yet. Wait until they've gone. I want to know what it would be like to kiss you, Joe Mannion.'

Chapter Seventeen

The Giudechina

'I've had the best possible afternoon,' said Ash, scraping up the last of her tiramisu.

'So have I,' said Joe. 'More than I could ever have imagined.'

And we've the rest of the evening, thought Ash. *And the night if we wanted it. Just the way Juliet arranged it.*

'Penny for them?' said Joe.

'Oh, I was just thinking,' lied Ash, 'about how it's all worked out for you, Joe, hasn't it?'

'All? I don't know about "all" of it yet. You sound as if you're sorry.'

'No, not sorry. I didn't mean it to come across like that. Envious, is probably closer.'

'You shouldn't be envious of money,' said Joe quietly.

'It's not the money. My problem is that if I'd had your good fortune when you had it, I don't think I'd have known what to do with it.'

'You sounded today as if you knew very well. I told you Professor Girotti was very impressed with you, and she can be difficult to please.' Then he added, in an altered voice, 'Look, do you really have to go back day after tomorrow? You couldn't just stay on a bit longer?'

'I will come back, Joe, but if I don't go now and find the kind of job I really want to do – if it really exists – then I'd end up settling for second best again just in order to be working. I mightn't be successful, but I have to try. I don't think my landlord has got wind of the fact I'm working temporary contracts and I'd rather have a new permanent job before he does. If it works out, then I'm sure I'd be able to find reasons to come here regularly. I could help set up internships for London gallerists or conservators with Professor Girotti. Omigod, Joe, I can hardly believe I am talking like this. As if *I* can make things happen.'

Joe put his hand over hers. Ash thrilled to his touch. His hand was large, warm, with a benign strength.

'You can. Like when you said you wanted to know what it would be like to kiss me. God, Ash, that was *so* good! Hell, with everything set up for me, I was still afraid of failing – of you rejecting me.' said Joe. 'Yet I've managed to do other stuff, though right enough, things "working out" as you put it, made it a hell of a lot easier. I wonder, in a way, if it's something about this place. You'll probably think I'm mad – I have no idea if what I am going to say would make any sense to you at all. There are times when I think Venice has to be a mirage. Somewhere so impossibly beautiful that you think you'll wake up from it. I even had the impression for the first few weeks I was here that I was on a boat, that water was shifting underneath me.'

'Perhaps it is.'

'Perhaps. They say this place was built on wooden staves driven into mud flats. We might just float off into the lagoon at any moment, as if the city was just a giant raft.'

'My life was like that, Joe, before I came here. I was just floating about, with no paddle and no idea of where I was going.'

'That feller you had, Ash. I'm sorry, I've forgotten his name again, though I did once make it my business to find out. Is he truly out of the picture?' Ash felt his hand gently release hers.

'He's truly out of the picture. In fact the picture fell off the wall, the frame was broken and it all went for firewood. It was a horrible old daub in the first place. Ed hasn't been my feller for ages. Only I forget how long because of the way Covid concertinaed time. He was bad news. I don't know if he's the reason I had no idea where I was going or if I stuck with him because I didn't know where else to go. Either way I shouldn't blame him. I'm an educated adult, allegedly.'

'So, I wasn't madly wanting to kiss his girl all this time,' Joe said.

'Not all of the time.'

'Hey,' he murmured. 'I'm sorry for talking about you as if you were some other man's property.'

Ash wanted to say that she wished he'd tried back in the Gulliver and Brant days but knew perfectly well that she'd have turned down dull Joe from Accounts, whether Ed had been there or not. She looked down at her empty plate.

'Don't be.'

'This is marvellous, Ash. Making up for three wasted years.'

'Don't tell me you were pining after me that whole time?'

Joe's expression darkened. 'Yes – and no.' He sighed. 'My life is a bit more complicated than I ever let on.' She saw him draw back a little.

'So you've a backstory too, Joe?'

'I have. Doesn't everybody?'

'Are you wanting to tell me?'

'I didn't tell anyone the whole time it lasted. I couldn't.'

'Is it properly over, Joe?'

'It is. More than a year ago. I shan't be seeing her again and I wouldn't want to.'

'She's not why you're here?'

'No. Not at all. She's abroad herself now.'

'Oh, where?'

'Bermuda, last I heard.'

'Bermuda? She'll run into old Brant then, if she's unlucky.'

'She won't run into him, Ash. She's *with* old Brant. She never had any intention of being with anyone else.'

Ash stared at him, her mouth open, until Joe put a finger under her chin and gently raised her jaw.

'So *that's* why you tore a strip off him on Zoom? And that's what Wanda was doing on Hampstead Heath?'

'We were done by then, honestly. Bar the shouting. But Rupert deserved it anyway. I mean, me tearing a strip off him *and* his wife cheating with me. Not that I'm proud of the cheating bit. There, that's the only dirty secret I have to tell you. The rest is pretty tedious. Joe in Accounts, you know.'

'I'd never have guessed.'

'Nobody would. That's what made it all so easy. And because it was easy, more difficult to get out of.'

'How long did it last?'

'A year, maybe? A bit less.'

'And it's really over?'

'God yes. I'm not just saying that because I want us to kiss again.'

Ash kept telling herself it was 'only' the local bus service, but there was something exhilarating about sitting in the prow of the line 2 vaporetto back to Piazza San Marco, with Joe's arm around her. He leaned in, talking to her, but she didn't initially hear him over the chug of the engine. She turned her face towards him; their mouths close.

'I was saying, it's hard to choose where we can kiss

again. Any little bridge in Venice is a romantic setting, but the garden of the villa is a hard act to follow.'

Ash smiled in reply, quickly brushing his lips with her own. It wasn't quite a kiss, more the promise of one. She drew back as quickly.

'Where are you taking me now, Joe?' She realised, from the way he swallowed, that he had become nervous.

'Um... wherever you like. We could go for a walk. Or perhaps you'd like to go back to your hotel. Or I could show you where I live.'

'Let's go for a walk, just to shift that tiramisu a bit. Then you could show me your flat. And I could meet Hetty.'

They paused at the marble façade of the church of San Zulian, letting the crowds of the Merceria flow past them.

'What is it, Joe?'

'I just wanted to stop and tell you what this means to me. I love being in Venice. I think there's nowhere in the world I'd rather be. I thought life here couldn't be better here than it was. But being here with you takes everything to a whole new level. You see, I'd sort of archived ever being with you.' He pulled her closer, his hand holding her head against his heart. She marvelled at the solidity of him, the sense of strength that emanated from him. She felt his lips on her hair, a gesture so tender she thought she might cry. But she hoped he wasn't going to kiss her then. It was too public.

'Shall we walk on?' he murmured.

As they turned away, Ash glanced up at the façade of the church. Above the door, a bronze statue of a man looked down on them, holding what looked like a book in one hand and a plant in the other.

'Who's he?'

'He was a doctor,' said Joe. 'I can't remember his name offhand, but it'll be somewhere in that inscription; my Latin isn't up to much. But I read that the plant he's holding was a remedy, if you can call it that, for syphilis and yellow fever.'

'I thought yellow fever was a tropical disease.'

'If it is now, it wasn't always. We're lucky we live now, Ash, in many ways. There's an island out in the lagoon – it's an art space now – that used to be a leper colony. And there are at least two churches built to mark the end of outbreaks of plague. That big one called the Salute.'

'Meaning health,' said Ash, pleased with herself.

'Exactly. And the church we were close to today, near Villa Hériot, Il Redentore – the Redeemer.'

'Covid was a plague,' said Ash. 'Us all staying indoors, afraid of human contact. And those scenes of undertakers struggling to cope – or Italian army lorries taking the dead from hospitals to morgues.'

'Bring out your dead,' murmured Joe. His hand held hers more tightly.

'Juliet's nan died. She didn't even get the chance to say good-bye to her.'

Joe swore softly. 'Poor Juliet. I didn't know.'

'Our holiday was partly in memory of her. Juliet's going to name her new business after her.'

Chapter Eighteen

Cannaregio

As they walked through Campo Santa Maria Formosa Ash felt an urge to wave in the direction of the webcam, wondering how many people were watching their two stick figures crossing in front of the church.

'Come over here a minute,' said Joe. 'Here, where you found me sketching.'

'Was that really only a few hours ago? It feels like so much has happened since.'

'Because it has.' Standing to the right of the door, separated from it by a marble pilaster, Joe smoothed back Ashley's hair with both hands, and cupped her face.

'May I?' he asked, dipping his mouth to hers.

Afterwards, he said, 'Will I see you back home, or do you want to meet Hetty? It's sort of on the way.'

'Meet Hetty,' said Ash, though she knew the thumping

of her heart hadn't got much to do with being introduced to Joe's cat.

It took some time to get to Joe's home in the Cannaregio district, for they kept stopping, whenever they entered a narrow alleyway and found themselves alone. There were many opportunities; Ash marvelled at the way the main thoroughfares in Venice were thronged with people, but just a couple of turns into side alleys and silence reigned. Finally, Joe said, 'It's that house. The other side of the canal,' as they walked over the last bridge. 'It's so pretty!' exclaimed Ash, looking up at a pink-washed façade. The *piano nobile* had a row of the distinctive ogee arched windows so typical of Venice. She remembered he'd mentioned having an attic flat, though, and raised her eyes to the simple square windows of the last storey.

'Oh. Sorry, Ash, it's not that one. I'm next door – a bit more ordinary. But the pink house makes it easy to give directions. The painter Tintoretto lived there.'

'Oh yes. I see the plaque now. Is that a statue of him too?' she said, looking at the near-life sized Istrian stone statue of a turbaned man set into a squint niche between Tintoretto's house and its neighbour.

'Ah, no. He was probably a spice merchant. This is Fondamenta dei Mori, and that's Campo dei Mori just round there, the place of the moors. There are other statues, see, supposed to be his brothers. That one on the corner has an iron nose as he lost his marble one. You're meant to touch it for luck.'

'I don't need luck, now. I've all the luck I need.'

'Oh Ash!'

'So this is your house?' Ash looked up at a more modest building; she vaguely remembered from a school art class that the faded colour of its façade was called something like Burnt Sienna. 'This is where one day they'll put up a plaque to the famous restorer Joe Mannion?'

'I think you have to be dead for that as well as famous. So not yet, I hope.'

'That's your terrace, is it, up there?'

'Yes. My studio looks onto it. But my bedroom is where those two windows are, and there's a door onto the terrace, so I take my first coffee of the day out there. Oh, it looks as if we're expected. Hetty, no jumping!'

A little cat – Ash could see she was white with some indeterminate blotches - was stepping delicately along the balustrade of the terrace. Hearing her name, she turned a heart-shaped face to the two looking up at her and chirped a greeting.

'Hello, furry-bird. You're a cat, remember?' he called up. Then he took out a key. 'This one's my front door.'

'What was here?' asked Ash, looking at the shuttered shop on the ground floor.

'I don't know. I think it's been like that for years. I've been toying with the idea of getting in to look inside. It might make a good workspace, or an art gallery. It might even be an investment. Venice has this scheme for digital nomads – Venywhere, it's called – to help people move here for six months or so to live and work.'

'I'd not want to leave after six months.'

'Well, I wouldn't either. But I'm glad you think so too.' He opened the street door onto a narrow staircase. 'I'm on the last floor,' he said, 'but for Hetty and me it's the best one.'

Ash followed him up; Joe filled the space.

'It's a great place for a cat,' he was saying. 'The rooftops are her world, but she goes down to street level as well. We even go for little walks. No cars, of course, but sometimes I worry about her stowing away on a barge, especially if it's a fisherman's.' He glanced round. 'You're still there? I'm burbling, sorry. Fact is, I'm nervous.'

So am I, thought Ash, *but in a good way.*

The gloom of the narrow stair gave way to the luminous space of Joe's flat. Ash looked round, taking in framed paintings she recognised as Joe's, from their similarity to what she had seen of his sketchbook, interspersed with old engravings of Venice in its prime as a city of pleasure. Amongst some modern, pale pine furniture, were some older pieces, not gleaming antiques but plain, sturdy items that looked as though they had seen service in a farmhouse. Everything was spotlessly tidy and clean, as was her glimpse of a little galley kitchen. Somewhere though, there was the oily scent of something else, something unusual in that orderly setting.

'I keep it this way,' said Joe, following her gaze. 'It makes a change from the studio.' Joe opened a door onto an organised chaos of easels, half-finished paintings, a guddle of tubes of paint and chipped jars stuffed with brushes. This was obviously the source of the smell – Ash recognised it now as a mixture of linseed oil and turpentine. Floor-length windows faced the terrace, some of them open to the sunshine; Ash looked out on a distinctive Venetian skyline of tiled roofs, chimneypots looking like buckets on stalks, other secret rooftop patios trimmed with geraniums. The roof too was of glass, but with blinds that could be pulled across, as in hot weather it would be an oven otherwise.

'It's wonderful, Joe. It's a dream. Oh, hello Hetty.' Ash bent down to stroke the cat who was winding herself against her legs. In response, Hetty sat up momentarily on her back paws, head-butting Ash's hand.

'She's beautiful, Joe. Will she let me pick her up?'

'I think she's expecting it.'

Ash bent over, gathering up the cat in her arms. In response, the little body thrummed with purrs. Ash looked into eyes of a startling blue, matching the afternoon sky.

'Cats know,' murmured Joe. He was smiling. 'That's if she is a cat. She's so tiny. I have this theory that she escaped from a Danish mink farm when she knew the game was up, got some novelty cat ears off eBay and stowed away on a ship in Esbjerg or somewhere and eventually made her way to the cat shelter at Malamocco which is where I found her.'

Ash laughed. 'Well, she'll never tell us. Will we finish the tour, Joe?'

'This way.'

Another door opened on Joe's bedroom. It was painted a pristine white, bar the dark beams that crossed the ceiling. The bedding too was crisp white, though Ash was puzzled that though Joe had a double-bed, it had two single duvets. Through a partly-open sliding door, Ash glimpsed a bathroom. The bedroom floor was paved in a checker-pattern of coral-pink Verona marble and creamy Istrian stone, that Ash recognised from countless churches and museums across the city. The only other colour was a simple kilim rug by the bed, and the dark wood of the headboard.

'It's an old piece of panelling. I just hung it there; the bed is new.'

'The engraving is old too?'

It was the only picture in the room and it hung above the bed, depicting a solemn Madonna and a very convincing baby. It looked familiar to Ash.

'That was probably produced for tourists in the nineteenth century. It's what's called a chromolithograph. A sort of tinted photograph. The original is in the Accademia.'

Ash remembered. 'Jules and I saw it. It's a Bellini.'

Joe looked delighted. 'I found it in Portobello Road Market. Coals to Newcastle, as they say. I never imagined at the time that I'd ever hang it on my own wall here in Venice. But then there's lots I didn't imagine I'd do in life, let alone here.'

As if on cue, Hetty wriggled out of Ash's arms and scuttled out of the room.

'Ash?'

Joe was standing very close to her now. She could hear the tension in his breathing – or was it her own? His dark eyes held hers intently. Ash saw longing in their depths, and something like fear. She wanted the fear to go away.

'Joe,' she said, putting her hand to his cheek. His mouth turned to kiss the hand fleetingly, then closed in on her own.

The kiss finished only with the promise of more. Joe cradled her head, his cheek against his, his breathing thunder in her ear, his body urgent.

'Ash?' he whispered.

'Mmm…'

'Can I? Omigod, just tell me if it's too soon. Can I be inside you?'

'Yes… yes,' she said, as his lips ranged across her face, below her ear.

'I don't mean straightaway, if you don't want to. I mean, we can take our time. I'd want to… I have waited and dreamed about this for so long.'

It's not just because it's so long since I've had sex, though it is. I'm going home on Thursday and I don't know if I'll get another chance. I just knew as soon as we kissed that I wanted him.

'I do. I do want this. I want you, Joe.'

Those unrepeatable moments of discovery followed, hands fumbling at each other's buttons, the touching of skin for the first time as a shirt was pulled from a waistband, a bra unclipped - though not without a nervous laugh from Joe. 'I'm not that good at this bit, am I?' he said, as his fingers fumbled under her t-shirt. Ash was glad he wasn't. The last catch unhooked, he eased t-shirt and bra over her head and with a low 'oh! of appreciation bent to kiss her breasts.

When he raised his head again to kiss her mouth, Ash pushed his unbuttoned shirt off his shoulders and ran her hands over his torso. She couldn't help but think of Ed, the last man she had touched and because she had been so long with him, the last man she really remembered. Joe wasn't rock-hard and glossy, like Ed, but he had the leanness of a man who walked a lot, and the texture of his skin and the whorls of dark hair around his nipples made him feel real. His heart felt to her closer to the surface, and so more vulnerable. Her hands travelled down, fluttering at his belt buckle.

'Do you mind if I...?' murmured Joe in her ear.

'Mind what?' she whispered.

'Put my hand up your skirt.'

'No... I'd mind if you didn't.'

His fingers had the deftness of a man used to patient, painstaking work.

'Oh, Ash. I've wanted to do that for so long.'

Ash said nothing, for she wasn't sure in her aroused state how her voice would come out. She wasn't even sure if she *could* speak. With his other hand, Joe tugged at his zip, to Ashley's relief, for she wasn't sure how she would have got it down without hurting what pressed urgently against it. Joe freed himself, quite roughly, Ash thought. It was odd how men could be like that with their own bodies.

'Wait a moment,' said Joe huskily. He lay her gently on the bed and pulled down the last of her clothes.

'Oh, Ash!'

She used one foot against the other to ease off her sandals, which fell on the pile of clothing with a muffled thump.

'I can't make love to you wearing my socks,' said Joe, bending to pull them off. Then he added a question. 'Protection?'

'Don't need it.'

Ash stretched out on the bed in anticipation as a naked Joe leaned over her. She expected him to enter her straightaway, but instead she felt the soft brush of his hair on her neck, breasts and stomach. Then Joe murmured, 'I'm a gentleman. She comes first,' and gently made sure that she did.

Much later, they drew apart, skin glowing with clean sweat, the two duvets entangled like wrestlers at the foot of the bed, Ash marvelling at how such large, strong hands had proved to be so sensitive, Joe's mouth even more so – and at how good the smell of him was.

Ash propped herself on her elbow, looking down at Joe. She loved the contrast of his dark hair against the stark white of the pillow. More than that, she loved his look of astonished happiness. She knew she didn't have much to compare it with, remembering Ed in these moments as either being hellbent on 'more' or already thinking about something else.

Why am I even thinking about Ed? He so doesn't count anymore. All I know is that I just want to go on seeing Joe like that. Always and always.

'What is it, Ash?' said Joe, looking suddenly anxious.

'Oh, nothing. Only that I like being with you like this, Joe.'

'That's not nothing. That's everything. C'mere.' He reached his arms out to her and pulled her against the length of him. She revelled in the warmth, the solidity of him.

'Like this,' he said, moving her pliant body until she straddled him.

'*Ohh...*' His hands went from her waist to her hips to her bottom. 'Oh, Ash, like that.'

'Why didn't you want the *preservativo?*' he asked afterwards.

'The what?' said Ash, startled, thinking about apricot jam.

'Sorry. I meant the condom. I had to go and look that word up before I went to buy them.'

'*Preservativo*. I suppose that is a better name. It describes what it does. I'm on the pill, Joe. It's to control heavy periods.'

'Oh, you poor thing.'

Ash's head jerked up, surprised at the kindness in his voice.

'I've not told anyone about that before – apart from Mum, and Juliet, of course.'

'Not Ed?'

'No. He never wanted to know stuff like that.'

'Sod him,' said Joe angrily.

'Let's forget him. I have. It's funny I was able to tell you without thinking about it. As if I'd known you forever.'

'You have.'

'Not really. I never saw the real you, I think.'

'I saw you the whole time. I couldn't take my eyes off you or stop thinking about you. Even, if I'm honest, when I was with Wanda Brant. Which of course made everything more difficult between her and me, even if I never let on.'

Ash wanted to ask, 'Did you love her at all?' But she held the words in her throat, waiting. Joe was silent, though, so eventually she said, 'I can't quite imagine you with her. I didn't meet her often, but she always looked so glossy. All that designer stuff she wore.'

'Yep. A bit like a Christmas tree. Well, as you've probably noticed, I'm *not* glossy. I was her bit of rough, really, and she was bored. I was also afraid of what she might do if I said no. I can't say I was enjoying myself with her but I didn't want to start looking for another job to get away from her because I'd not get to see you either; talk about being caught between a rock and a hard place! But I'd be lying if I said it didn't give me a bit of a thrill to get one over Rupert Brant, sleeping with his trophy wife.'

'Did anyone else know you were?'

'Well, if they did, it's not because *I* told them. It did cross my mind that she'd chosen me because I was the last person Brant would suspect, but since it ended I've wondered if he didn't even set the whole thing up himself.'

'Guh!'

'Quite. I wouldn't put it past her to have gone home and told him how I performed. Whatever turns you on. I always used to use condoms with her, Ash, but that wasn't because I didn't trust her. It was because I didn't trust *him*. By the time I gave out to him on that Zoom call I don't think I cared if he knew or not. I knew Rupert needed me at the end. He was bullying poor Cora over the size of the redundancy payments, but he hadn't a clue about the sums, not really, and his idea of ethics was just not to get caught. He was forever trying to get me to do things that wouldn't have been quite legal, only because they suited him. I always refused. He'd grumble until I laid out for him, once again, what the penalties would be. It was a bit like what working for Trump must've been like, or Elon Musk, Poundshop version. When Wanda broke with me, I was put out – a man's got his pride, after all – but deep down I was relieved – well, not that deep down, if I'm honest. Just say you'd given me a glimmer of hope back then, Ash, a sign that you might have liked me. It would have been bloody difficult to have got myself out of that situation with her and still have a job. But she started ghosting me after I'd had a particularly tough talk with Brant about why he couldn't put something or other against tax so I think it might've been his way of throwing his toy out of the pram.'

At that point the bedroom door, which Joe had been too distracted to close properly, was nosed open and with a chirp and a blur of white fur, Hetty landed on the bed and began a charm offensive on Joe.

'Rough tongue!' exclaimed Joe, screwing up his face as the cat tried to lick his nose and eyelids. He sat up and cuddled her.

'She does this in the mornings when she wants breakfast. All right, little lady,' he added, addressing the cat. 'You've been really discreet all this time and I shouldn't have been talking about the Brants anyway, today of all days. I've prosecco in the fridge, Ash. What if we have a glass on the terrace and you tell me if you want me to see you home.'

'Do I have to go home?'

'Well, I'd rather you didn't.'

'I'll go back for breakfast then, and fresh clothes.'

'Don't talk about putting clothes on – not just yet.'

Joe put his arm around her from behind, nuzzling her neck. Two glasses clinked dangerously in his other hand. Ash wriggled round, unfurling a flute from his fingers.

'Don't wake me up,' she said. 'This skyline. The long shadows at the end of a perfect day. Hearing the footsteps of the people going home – this city is still alive and you're a part of it.'

'Hold your horses, Ash. You don't know what kind of cook I am yet. Would you have dinner with me here, tomorrow, to find out?'

Chapter Nineteen

27th April: last full day

It hadn't been easy disentangling herself from Joe's arms that morning, but Ash had insisted.

'I'll eat with you tonight, but I'll go home afterwards. We've an early start for the airport.'

Joe raised himself on his elbow in the tumble of bedlinen. Ash looked at him, with his tousled hair, his dark eyes, and asked herself how she could ever have thought he was boring.

I think I might be falling in love. Or am I just in love with the idea of being in love?

'All right. But promise me you'll be back soon.'

Ash sighed. 'I want to be.' *But I want to know how real this is first.*

'There'll be the wedding, of course.'

'They've got a date?'

'They do. October.'

'Oh.' *Aren't we going to see each other before then?*

'Earliest they could make it. I was brought up a Catholic, remember,' said Joe. 'You have to give a minimum of six months' notice to the priest.'

'How did you know it was October?'

Joe smiled. 'As you know, I am part of a network of spies. I checked my messages when you were in the shower last night.'

'Jules!'

'Davide, actually, via Jules.'

'October, then,' said Ash, as casually as she could.

'I was planning on spending time with you before that, if you're agreeable. Like lunchtime, to start with.'

'That should be me and Juliet. But you can guess where we are going.'

'All right if I turn up for coffee?'

'I'd like that.'

Ash enjoyed the brief walk back to the hotel in the early morning. *Hardly any tourists about yet. Just dog walkers and people going to work. Makes me feel like I live here.*

As she neared the hotel, she saw a familiar figure scuttling along in front of her, wearing a distinctive pair of red shoes. She caught up enough to see Juliet stifle a huge yawn, but to stand back as the man of the breakfast room German couple came out, trying to light a cigar.

'Morning!' said Juliet.

'*Morgen*!' said the man in astonishment, dropping his

cigar. It was obvious from his expression that he realised a somewhat sleepy and rumpled Juliet had indeed been out all night. As he bent to pick it up, Juliet slipped past him and up the stairs.

'*Morgen*!' said Ash, as he straightened up. Seeing her, he muttered something like '*Auch die Andere.*'

'Excuse me,' said Ash, taking the cigar out of his mouth and putting in back in the correct way round.

Fifteen minutes later a somewhat spruced up Juliet and Ash took their places at the breakfast table, smelling of hotel soap. The proprietor bustled over at once with their coffee, grinning from ear to ear.

'Good night, was it, hun?' said Juliet.

'The best. And you?'

'Yup.'

'Verdict on Venice?'

'The best.' Juliet raised her hand and Ash followed in a high-five.

On the other side of the breakfast room, Ash saw the German couple get to their feet, the man scraping back his chair and his wife dutifully following him out. The man's nose was in the air. He exuded disgust.

A moment later, the wife reappeared, going back to her table. Ash watched her. She seemed to be looking for something but not very effectively. *Pretending,* thought Ash, trying not to stare. Then the woman glanced over her shoulder, towards the entrance, as if to check she wasn't being watched.

'Jules!' said Ash in a stage whisper. 'Cigar-man's wife is coming this way.'

'What—'

'*Toll, toll! Viel Glück!*' exclaimed the woman, with a look of glee that made her seem ten years younger. She patted first Juliet and then Ash on the arm and then scuttled off before they could say anything.

'Do you know any German, Jules?'

'Nope, but I am pretty sure she wants some of what we've been having.'

'You're not just a great lay,' Ash heard herself say, after swallowing her first mouthful of dinner. 'You're a talented cook, too.'

'Oh! Thank you. But I'm a cheat – about the cooking, anyway. Everything else, Ash, was as good as I could make it. The tortellini fresh from a shop round the corner. With a glass of wine and freshly grated parmesan even I can't fail. I should have blagged that I'd shaped the cases and stuffed them myself. Most of the time I just go to Conad and buy the ones in the plastic packets. Please don't look in my fridge, Ash. Italy doesn't go much for convenience foods, but what they do have, I've got.'

'You bought this for me, then.'

'Guilty. Accountants are planners.'

'Is the two duvet thing a planning thing too?'

'Oh... yes, I suppose so. And thanks for straightening them out this morning. I used to share a flat with a German lad. He said nobody in Germany had double duvets even on double beds. Everyone gets their own, so there's no fighting, and generally you sleep better. So being a planner, I bought a double bed, because, you know, hope and that...'

'I do.'

He looked out across the rooftops at the pink dusk. 'But ever since Juliet messaged me and said you'd be in Campo Santa Margherita that time, I've laid the second duvet on the bed too. I... this is going to sound like I'm losing it, Ash... I'd lie there at night and have all these conversations with you.'

'Oh, Joe.' Her eyes filled. Ash couldn't remember anyone saying anything quite as tender as that to her, ever. 'I wish I didn't have to go away in the morning. Find that job. Face reality.'

'Is this not reality?' he said, gesturing at the skyline. 'Go back, Ash. Find the job that means you can be here, with me. Remember what Professor Girotti said. But can I come and see you in London?'

'I thought you'd never ask.'

'Tell me we're a Thing, Ash.'

'We're a Thing.'

'I love you, Ash.'

'I think you're persuading me to love you too, Joe Mannion.'

'I should go back to the hotel,' said Ash eventually.

'Can I walk you back?'

'I'd like that.'

Nestled against him as they walked, Ash asked hesitantly, 'Did you think I was a bit forward?'

'What, the not-going-to-bed-with-him-the first-night thing? I never thought of it that way. I'm just deliriously glad that you did. I feel like I've wasted so much time already, then Covid being a matter of life and death, literally. Not knowing when we'd be back to normal, whatever normal is, or what they kept calling 'the new normal' would look like. This was our world war, Ash. Events as big as that change how we think and behave, don't you think? *Carpe diem* again. And besides, I love you. I couldn't wait to show you how much. And then you showed it me back, and how! I so don't want you to go back on that plane. If you see someone charging across the airstrip and forcing it to stop tomorrow, it'll be me.'

Ash laughed, burying her face in his shoulder. *I can't get enough of the smell of him, or his solidity. How could I not have really seen him before?*

Ashley opened the door on an empty room. She undressed

reluctantly in the little bathroom and as reluctantly got into the shower, unwilling to wash Joe off, for lovemaking had inevitably followed the meal, but the habit of a nightly shower wasn't an easy one to break.

She lay on the narrow bed in the near dark gazing up at the ceiling, running through every incident of the events of the last couple of days. When she woke, she wasn't sure what time it was or quite where she was, instinctively reaching for Joe. But a sliver of light from a lamp bracket filtered through the shutters brought her back to reality. The scuffling at the door could not be Hetty wanting to leap onto the bed.

Outside, keys were dropped on the tiled floor, accompanied by a muffled curse. Finally the light round the edge of the door widened, and Ash made out Juliet's outline and heard the slap of bare feet on tiles. Sandals dangled from one of her hands.

Ash deliberately stirred.

'Shit! Did I wake you?' said Juliet in a stage whisper.

'I don't know. It doesn't matter. Let me put the light on.'

'Oh fuckety fuckety fuck,' said Juliet. 'I don't want to go home tomorrow. Have we any of that Cynar left? I don't know about you, but having over-indulged in all legal ways possible – fine food, wine and sex afterwards, I mean – I think I probably need a *digestif*.'

An hour later, with the glasses from the bathroom drained and sticky with liqueur, Ash and Juliet reluctantly called it a night. They liked the little hotel but didn't like the fact that their laughter had been loud enough for the person next door to rap on the wall.

'Ah, Venice,' whispered Jules from the neighbouring bed. 'It didn't let us down, did it?'

'No. Now it's up to us not to let Venice down either. For us to finish what it started,' said Ash. 'Joe said he'd be at the airport in the morning.'

'I know. He told Davide. He'll be there too. Fist bump?'

Ash swung out her arm.

Chapter Twenty

As Ash had feared, Venetian dreams weren't easy to hold onto, though they were always there, just out of the corner of her eye. In the rush of feet on wet, crowded pavements, she remembered how her footsteps and Joe's had synchronised on that first walk from Campo Santa Maria Formosa to his home. She became a regular in the Italian rooms at the National Gallery, seeking to recapture the light and colour of the city in paintings she wished she was looking at with Joe. In the Victoria and Albert, reading the label for a sculpture of the Virgin Mary sheltering a lot of little men in hoods under her cloak, she realised that it had been torn from the façade of an old confraternity building only a few paces from Joe's door.

She registered again for contract work, but deliberately avoided anything that looked like a long-term proposition. Some of it was interesting. Some of it was just stuffing folders and putting the name tags on lanyards.

'I like the mundane jobs better, in a way,' she told Joe on Zoom. 'It means I can do them on automatic and think about you instead.'

On Saturdays, she helped Jules set up *Lucia*. The shop was coming on leaps and bounds. Ash organised the social media accounts, with the help of a design student in need of a final year project. From Venice, Gianni helped with the website. 'Donatella is handling the wedding preparations,' he explained. 'I am just keeping out of the way.'

The local newspaper ran a feature on *Lucia*. 'It must be a slow news day,' was Juliet's cheerful comment.

'I've never had such fun with a launch,' was Ashley's.

'Don't forget your own plans, girl,' said Juliet through a mouth full of pins. She was in the middle of arranging a gorgeous 1950s party dress on a battered vintage manikin. Ash had seen the 'before' pictures of this dress: the original lace overlay had been torn beyond redemption, but the artificial shot silk beneath had survived more or less intact. The new lace had come from an end of line bolt discovered in the backshop of a fabric store that had closed down.

Juliet made her last adjustments and spat the remaining pins into her hand. 'There. Not bad, though I say it myself.' She placed the framed 'before' photograph of what had looked like a ruin next to the manikin's feet.

On Sundays, Ash went with her Oyster card up to town and walked, reading buildings in a way she had never thought to do until Joe had shown her why Villa Hériot was a pastiche, though a beautiful one. In a near deserted City of London, she found a Victorian building that wouldn't have looked out of place on the Grand Canal, its doorway looking as if it was the entrance to a church, with pretty ogee arches above. She WhatsApped a photo of it to Joe. He sent a selfie back – him and Davide outside the restaurant.

'That feels like home,' she murmured. But how to get back there seemed to recede by the minute.

'Let's get down to business,' said Jules, from behind her sewing machine. She was replacing a torn ruffle on a cardigan with a bright spotty one found on Etsy. '*Your* business. I know you've got work and it's always easier to get a job from a job, but the great resigners or whatever they're called will come back eventually either because they're bored or because they're poor. Now is the best time to find the job you really want.'

'It was easy to talk about it while I was in Venice. Everything seemed possible then. Under a rainy London sky it doesn't. I got plenty of responses to those CVs I sent out, but really it was just more of what I'd done before.'

'Yet everybody thinks of London like it's paved with gold. See that pencil and paper, Ash? Start googling all the galleries you might possibly be able to work in and the impossibles too. Then we'll go and check them out together.'

'Meaning?'

'Meaning you walk in and hand them your CV.'

'Gulp. But I don't have anything to wear. My business suits are all pretty trad.'

'Your business suits are dull,' said Jules.

Ash winced.

'But *you* aren't dull,' said her friend. 'And *we* have *loads* to wear,' she added, waving an expansive arm at the growing racks of clothes. 'Block a day in the next fortnight and I'll do the same.'

Ash had to admit she felt the business, looking at herself in the cheval glass. It was a moment like the time she had tried on the Burano lace dress in the store at Santa Maria Mater Domini. That was the fun Ash, the carefree Ash, the Ash who was ready to fall in love – properly this time. As she had – she thought it might be a bit weird telling Joe so when all she had of him was a slightly washed-out Zoom image – but it wasn't. And here was another Ash, in a vintage Dior suit in sober dark fabric, an Ash that meant to be taken seriously. It was the cut that gave the wide skirt and the fitted jacket their verve, embellished by the Richard Allen scarf with its pops of red, brown and cream colour in a geometric design and a Birkin style handbag. The Venetian glacé Mary-Janes gave the ensemble just that hint of playfulness that stopped her outfit from being too sober.

'I just feel a bit self-conscious,' she said to Juliet. 'Can I really go out looking this elegant?'

'Course you can. I'll be in seventies snazz. It'll help you look more serious.'

By the time the two had come up from the Underground at Bond Street, Ash reckoned they'd been photographed at least twice. She began to relax, to preen even, whenever she caught her reflection in a plate glass shop window. She'd been afraid of derisory looks, but what they got were frankly admiring glances. That too reminded her of Venice. People liked clothes there. They wanted to look properly put together, as if that mattered, and they liked looking at how other people dressed.

'Go, girls!' called out a couple of teenage girls, 'you look *wicked*!' Then a Chinese tourist raised his camera.

The job hunt didn't go quite so well to start with.

'Ew naio' said a nasal young woman in the first gallery Ash entered. 'We only hire people we know,' she added, taking in Ash's clothes with ill-disguised jealousy.

'We didn't want that one anyway, did we?' said Jules as they pushed the street door open. 'Pity we wasted precious time looking at those horrible paintings first.'

In another, Ash and Jules were taken for buyers.

'I am sure you will agree that the artist speaks for all of us,' said the young man with the quiff, gesturing with fervour at a canvas plastered with what looked to Jules like impenetrable mud. 'A metaphor for the Zeitgeist, don't you think?' From there it could only go downhill. It didn't help that beyond the young man's shoulder Jules was making faces and pushing her hands between her thighs. Then mercifully, the youth paused, carried away with his own rhetoric. He shut his eyes and breathed in deeply, pressing his hands together. Ash wondered if this was a zen move.

'Um, I'm really sorry to interrupt, but do you have a bathroom?'

His eyes flicked open. 'A bathroom?' he said. From the look on his face, Ash wondered if this might be the name assumed by an up-and-coming performance artist. Then he said, 'Oh, you mean a *bath*room.' Bath was drawled, to rhyme with awl.

He turned round, flicked his fingers at an unmarked door, and Jules obediently scuttled off, shooting a warning look at Ash, who took the hint.

'I'm actually looking for a job.'

'Ew. You might have said.'

'I tried—'

'I don't think you'd do at all.'

'I've my CV, if you'd like to—'

'One is awfully busy, you know,' he said, gesturing at the empty gallery.

'I'll wait for my friend outside.'

The man opened the door for her, pointedly avoiding her eyes and her murmured 'Thank you' as she went out.

Juliet followed a moment later.

'I didn't need the bog. I just had to stop him somehow. I think we'll chalk that one up as a lucky escape.'

'We're being very lucky this morning then,' said Ash in a flat voice. 'I've not got anywhere near talking about the Villa Hériot. Nobody's even wanted to look at my CV. All my plans – let's call them dreams, as that's all they are – are turning into a mirage. At least you've managed to hand out some business cards.'

'I'm not sure if any of this lot are going to make that trip. Let's try one more, then go and get a beer. Who else is on your list?'

'There's this one, in a back street.'

Figgs & Son proved to have been an old butcher's shop. It occupied a corner site, with a preserved Victorian frontage which included the curly head of a bull complete with nose ring over the front door. It was impossible to see in; blinds obscured the windows. There was a doorbell, above a small brass plaque bearing the legend 'James Figgs, art dealer and conservator.' It took so long for it to be answered that Ash looked at her watch, wondering if it was lunchtime already.

'Time flies when you're enjoying yourself,' said Jules laconically.

In that moment the door was opened by a distinguished looking man in his forties, in baggy corduroys, highly polished brogues, a cream and brown checked shirt and a knitted waistcoat with leather buttons. Ash's heart sank. He looked like his own parody of a posh Englishman – carefully curated expensive casual.

He inclined his head.

'Ladies, you are magnificent. As I assume you have not come to rob me, do come in.'

To forestall the inevitable rebuff, Ash immediately blurted, 'We've not come to buy anything.'

'I should think not. You haven't seen anything yet.' He stood back and the two girls meekly went in through an inner door.

'Oh!' said Ash. For almost a minute nobody spoke. Afterwards, Ash said to Jules, 'It was like going into a church, wasn't it? I'm not religious, or anything, but those marvellous things…'

'Figgs was watching you the whole time, though. Your silence was the best compliment you could give him.'

Figgs's shop was an antidote to all the expensive, pretentious art they had been turned away from that morning. The dipped light, that Ash realised from something Joe had said in a conversation about light monitors and hygrometers was to protect the artefacts, contributed to the church-like atmosphere. There were tiny medieval panel paintings, gleaming gold and red and lapis lazuli blue, exquisite ivory figures of the Virgin and child, which Figgs explained followed the curve of the tusk of the centuries-dead elephant, German wood-carvings of saints and a little plaque of the Crucifixion he particularly rhapsodised over, in what looked to Ash like a translucent, waxy marble. 'Nottingham alabaster, don't you know? These were exported all over Europe in the Middle Ages. They wouldn't be able to do it now, of course. It'd go the way of that cheesemaker chap that was in the news. Too much Brexit paperwork. Hey ho.'

'I wouldn't be able to sell anything if I worked here,' said Ash eventually. 'I don't know how you could part with any of it.'

'Funny you should say that. I've wept buckets over some items. My consolation is when they go to museums, where people can see them, not back into the hands of another private collector. I know my competitors think I am not as hard-nosed as I should be; I've been known to turn down rich industrialists, oil barons and any number of Russian oligarchs in favour of a public gallery. You said you weren't here to buy anything; might one ask why you have paid me a visit?'

Ash opened her mouth and shut it. Then she remembered Professor Girotti at Villa Hériot, and Joe saying how impressed she'd been. But a dealer who felt that way about the items that kept him in business in premises behind New Bond Street would understand that what she had experienced in Venice could be more than a dream. She managed to find the words.

'I was in Venice a couple of months ago,' she began.

'Admirable choice.'

'I don't know if you've heard of the conservation school—'

'On the Giudecca? I should think it my business to have heard of it.'

'Oh. Oh good. You see, I've a friend who is studying there...'

'Ah! You are seeking a post for this young lady?' Ash noted the slight lowering of his eyelids, the frisson of boredom. *Careful, you'll lose him before you've got him.*

'No, I... my friend... he lives in Venice now. He was an accountant and now he's retraining as a conservator. I don't think he wants to come back.'

'Wise fellow. Everything here is going to hell in a hand cart.'

'Well, I... um...' *Where was I?*

'Ashley works in Marketing and Events Management,' piped up Juliet. 'She makes things happen.'

'Does she indeed? I'm not sure if I am in need of "making things happen" as you put it. I take it you are in the same line of business?'

Ash saw Juliet flushing under the putdown but was proud of her for soldiering on.

'No, Mr Figgs, I am a vintage clothing dealer.'

The unpredictable Figgs then made an odd little old-fashioned bow. 'A colleague of sorts, then, though not a competitor. By your rigout, I would guess you are both walking publicity for your business, I take it? My compliments.'

'Thank you.'

Figgs turned back to Ash. 'So you've been to the Villa Hériot, I suppose?'

'I have. I met the director, Professor Girotti...' Feeling more confident, Ash pressed on, telling Figgs an edited version of her trip to Venice, carefully omitting any reference to webcams and small shaggy dogs. She gained confidence as she saw his head tilt to one side, his intentness.

'So you see, there could be all sorts of opportunities for... for... *what was that word Brant was always trotting out. Sounds like an 80s synth-pop band...*'

'Whatever you do, don't mention synergy,' said Figgs.
Phew.

'Only I have no real experience,' she said, skidding to a halt and inwardly cursing herself.

'Ah, but you do,' said Figgs. 'Just not in the art world. Tell me, what was your favourite painting in Venice?'

Here we go. The "what did you do on your holidays" question. He's polite, but not really taking me seriously after all. I'll answer him, anyway, and then we can make our excuses and get out of here.

She paused. *Get on with it.* 'It was a Carpaccio painting in the Accademia,' she said. 'I can't remember its exact title, but it's to do with a sick man being cured by a relic of the true cross, or something. Only that's incidental, really. It happens in one corner of the painting. The rest is really a portrait of Venice, when the Rialto Bridge was built of wood and looks really rickety, with an open bit at the top that looks as if you could fall through it, because it's like a medieval version of Tower Bridge – a drawbridge. There are all these gondolas with little cabin things on them. Felt-something.'

'Felze,' said Figgs. 'Go on.'

'There's a young man in one with a white dog (*careful, Ash*) and one of the gondoliers is black, only not in a Bridgerton sort of way. There must have been black people living and working in Venice for Carpaccio to have painted them – along with Arab merchants in turbans. And I love the chimney pots, and the lady beating a carpet out of a high window, because that's more important to her than anything miraculous. There's a crowd of richly dressed men with self-important expressions looking like they're probably Freemasons—'

Figgs laughed like a drain.

'— but they must be portraits of real people,' said Ash. 'I mean we'll never know for sure, but they just look as if they are.'

'They are. They'll be the members of the confraternity who commissioned the painting. I know the one you're talking about and congratulate you on both your choice and your eye for detail. I think we can address the problem you mentioned – the one you think you have but which I see no evidence of – about not having the "right" experience. I've had a series of people working here – what in my day they called Sloanes – posh girls, with History of Art degrees some of them but none of your fervour. All style and Prada loafers and names like the Honorable Lady Venetia Robespierre hyphen Ghastly but absolutely no substance. You're not an Honorable, are you?'

'Um, no…'

'But you are nevertheless honorable, I trust. Could you start a week on Monday?'

Ash gaped. Jules gave her a dig in the ribs.

'Yes – I mean, thank you. I'd love to… I… What would you like me to do?'

'Oh gosh,' said Figgs, scratching his head. 'I suppose you'd want a job title. Do you think you could turn up Monday week and have a look at what needs doing and we'd take it from there? I'd pay you, of course. I confess to never paying the Venetias. They came as interns. I'd have paid them if I thought they needed the money but it was obvious they didn't. Serves me right, really. You do get what you pay for, or rather, not pay for. Only you ought to have a contract, oughtn't you?' He frowned. 'There's just me here, though I think we'd rub along all right. No Human Remains person. No, that's not right, is it? Human *Resources*.'

'If it helps,' said Ash, 'I do know somebody who could help with that. She wouldn't be free but I'm sure she'd be reasonable.'

'Cora?' said Jules.

'Yes, Cora.'

'Splendid,' said Figgs. 'I thought you'd be the kind who'd get me sorted out, and you've started already. And that chap in Venice. The one who used to be a bean counter. You don't suppose he'd like to keep his hand in, given the... the circumstances? Do my books, I mean.' added Figgs, waving at his exhibits.

'He's coming over on Friday so we could ask him then.'

Chapter Twenty-one

Zooming in London, July 2022

'I can't tell you how much this means to me,' spluttered Cora over Zoom.

'You were the first person I thought of. I should warn you though, Figgs is pretty eccentric and appallingly badly organised.'

'Oh good,' said Cora, a gleam in her eye.

'So where've you been working?'

'Locum jobs still,' said Cora, dully. 'You always hope that one of the placements would think I'd done a good job and want to take me from the agency. Only I've been typecast, if that's the right word, as an expert in handling redundancies, so usually it's me and the security man with the keys are the last ones left. I can't say it's conducive to a good night's sleep.'

'Except you'd make sure it was done properly,' said Ash.

'Thank you, I do try. I don't think I'd have fitted in most of the places I went to anyway. I'm pretty sure they thought

I was boring. Not aligned with their culture, or something. That drives me nuts, you know, the way companies go on about culture, as if they think they're art patrons, or semi-religious, banging on about their 'mission' and going on 'retreats' when all they mean is a tedious team meeting in a dreary hotel.'

'You'll never hear any of that language with Figgs. He'd probably think you were talking about the Starship Enterprise or something in the Crimean War if you spoke like that to him. You're not boring, you're dependable.'

As she said those words, she thought of Joe.

'Joe Mannion was here at the weekend, by the way,' she heard herself say.

'Joe? What's *he* doing?'

'Jules and I met him in Venice. He's on an art conservator's course. Turns out he's really, really good at it.' *And not just at that,* Ash added mentally.

'Wow! Good for him! So, you just ran into him accidentally?'

'Well, I thought it was. Only it was a sort of stitch-up.'

Ash told her, first about the sighting near the university, then about finding him sketching outside Santa Maria Formosa, eating in Davide's restaurant, the visit to Villa Hériot, though omitting the hand-holding in the Giudechina and the walk across Venice to the rooftop apartment next to Tintoretto's house. She deliberately made absolutely no reference to webcams or little white dogs.

'I remember he told me he'd inherited something in Ireland,' said Cora. 'I wondered if he might go there.'

'No, but it meant he could buy a flat in Venice and pay for his course. He says he's not coming back.'

'But you said it was a stitch-up. Are you – tell me to shut up, Ash – I mean, you just know so much about him. Are you by any chance together?'

'Yes,' said Ash quietly. 'Juliet set us up, really. That's what best friends are for.'

On screen, Cora whooped. Ash had never seen her do that spontaneously, though they'd both had to make the obligatory North Korean noises at company briefings.

'Oh Ash, I am *so* pleased. He always adored you!'

'He told you?'

'Well, you could see it. But he told me anyway. He never thought you even saw him.'

Oh, I saw him eventually, thought Ash, remembering the warm tones of his skin against white sheets.

'I'm glad he was able to tell someone,' said Ash truthfully. 'And I'm glad it was you.'

'There wasn't really anyone else he could tell,' said Cora, 'him and me being the company misfits.'

'Hardly that,' said Ash. 'Brant wouldn't have hired either of you if he'd thought that.'

'Well, that's the funny thing,' said Cora. 'Brant *didn't* hire me. I thought it was a bit weird at the time, being interviewed by someone who didn't work there, didn't know anything about the job, but was one of the directors. Wanda Brant hired me.'

Cora shivered. Aside from the fact that it was pretty off for Brant not to bother his head about who he had working with him on the decisions that impacted his employees most, it also said a lot about what Wanda Brant's priorities were. Cora had described herself as dull, exactly the word Joe had used about himself. Wanda wanted dull women around her husband. It was just accidental, if dullness was listed as one of the 'desirable criteria,' that Cora had proved to be quietly competent and principled. *But Brant hired me and Juliet. Does that mean he took us for our looks, not because of what we could do?* Ash felt a bit sick.

'I expect she thought I'd be no threat to her,' Cora went on. 'I could have told her there is no way I would be, but I'd never told anyone what I'm about to tell you. Do you mind being the first person I come out to?'

Ash gaped at Cora. *People are never only what you think they are. Look at Joe. Now Cora. And hey, look at me.* 'I'm honoured, Cora, really I am,' she eventually said, reading Cora's look of dismay at her vacant expression. Ash found herself tearing up.

'Oh Cora, I am so sorry you've had to keep this to yourself for so long. What made you choose me?'

'It's because you're with Joe. And because you thought of me for that work with Mr Figgs. I had thought of telling

Joe, after he'd confided in me about you, but I still didn't have the courage.'

'You really never told anyone? Not even somebody in your family.'

'Especially not them.' Cora started to cry, great gulping sobs.

'I'm so, so sorry,' said Ash, wishing she could say something less conventional and more helpful. Most of all she wished she could put her arms around Cora. 'Do you want to talk about it?'

Cora blew her nose on one of her impeccably ironed handkerchiefs.

'They're really religious. Evangelicals. I'm sure not all Evangelicals are like them but they have really, really got it in for queer people. It's like it defines them. I know the Bible inside out but it took me a long time to find any reference to, you know, girl on girl. There's plenty of fire and brimstone stuff about boy on boy, but I did also find something St Paul said about women like me: "unnatural relations." Honestly, Ash, chance would be a fine thing.'

'I'm no expert, but this is St Paul, not Jesus, right?'

Cora pulled a wry face. 'Jesus says nothing about being queer. Nothing at all. There's one place where he tears into paedophiles.'

'Not the same thing.'

'Thank you. But when I tried to talk to Mum and Dad

they said they'd pray for me. Then they brought someone round to the house who said he could cure me.'

'You don't mean—'

'Not that. One of those conversion therapy courses. I left home two days later. Mum and Dad shouted at me for not *wanting* to be cured. I couldn't get them to see it wasn't a matter of wanting to, it was that I couldn't be cured – because I wasn't ill, or deviant. I was just me. That's when they were convinced the devil had got hold of me. It would have been exorcism next – never mind conversion therapy. Or perhaps that's just the modern version.'

'And now? Are you with someone now?'

Cora smiled, a really attractive, shy smile, Ash thought.

'Not yet. But I'm hopeful. I found a queer friendly church to go to – a different denomination. I've met someone I like there. I mean, all we've done is go for coffee afterwards, but she does seek me out.'

Carpe diem, thought Ash. 'Ask her out, Cora. She might be trying to get up the courage too. What's the worst can happen?'

'She says no, or she has someone already.'

'You won't know until you ask – or she does. In the meantime, come and meet Mr Figgs. Something to talk about on your first date.'

James Figgs did a doubletake on meeting Cora, as did she. Ashley looked from one face to the other, thinking *how many people live in London?*

'My dear lady,' he said, holding Cora's hand. 'What an unexpected pleasure this is. Ashley is a genius, I think. A necromancer, even. You usually sit by one of the pillars on the right-hand side, don't you? I've seen you with Sally afterwards. Might you be what they call "an item"?'

Cora had gone a rosy pink. 'I wish...'

'Leave it to me,' said Figgs expansively, 'I'm good at that kind of thing. It's the only kind of organisation I am good at, to be honest. As you are about to find out. Ashley here is in need of a job title, a contract, all the matters she tells me you are expert in...'

Chapter Twenty-two

'How long have you worked here, Ashley?' asked Figgs, handing over one of the two lattes he had gone out to buy.

'Only a matter of weeks. But I can't imagine working anywhere else.'

'Hmm, except Venice possibly, if you've any sense – and you do. Well, you're already transforming things, you and Cora and that man of yours. Between the three of you, you even saw off that chap from the Revenue. He was about to cut up rough. It's not that I don't want to pay my taxes, you understand, it's just that I can't make head nor tail of their forms – and as for Making Tax Digital. It might as well be Making Tax Demented as far as I'm concerned. Went off all smiles, he did. Complimented me on the professionalism with which I turned things round. Not that *I* can take any credit.'

Ash smiled patiently. It hadn't initially been easy, neither making sense of Figgs's paperwork, nor convincing the tax inspector that her employer was determined to put things on a more professional footing. It had been a lengthy process, but she'd triumphed in the end, though without fanfare. 'Speaking of credit,' she said, 'you're even due for small rebate.'

'Spend it,' said Figgs at once, without even asking how much it was. 'Buy a flight ticket with it, because I'm ordering you off the premises. Go and see Joe. Go and oil the wheels with Professor Girotti while you're at it.'

'But Joe is here this week. He'll be in later. The institute is closed for the summer and he says you can't move in Venice for tourists.'

'Oh yes, you did say.'

'And that second-year panel conservator is due in ten days.'

'So she is. I'd like her to look at that new arrival. Circle of Taddeo di Bartolo, I think. Only it's in poor condition. That wretched belted earl who brought it home in 1850 whatever it was hung it above his dining-room mantelpiece and put a candelabra beneath it. And then compounded the offence by getting one of his friends to retouch the faces.'

Ash shuddered.

Word had got round that James Figgs was coming to an arrangement with Villa Hériot. *The Art Quarterly* had already been in touch about doing a feature on the gallery and a photographer was lined up to do a shoot both there and in Venice. His competitors were sniffing around as well. Ash was on her own one morning, James having slipped out to buy them both coffee, when the doorbell rang. Through the intercom Ash recognised her caller.

Ash recounted what happened next not only to Figgs, who came in as the caller left, 'with sparks flying in all directions' as he put it, but also that evening to Juliet and Joe over a pizza in Don Luigi's.

'Do you remember that first gallery we went into, where that up-herself female told us that they only worked with "people we know?"'

'How could I forget,' said Juliet. 'I don't know which was worse, her or the paintings.'

'She turned up this morning. "I don't believe we've met. Figgs's temp, are you?" she drawls at me. "Oh, we've met, and I am not a temp," I said. She peered at me. "The Ivy, was it?" "Nope." "That private view at the Royal Academy, then." "I was there," I said, "but I never noticed you." "Is Mr Figgs in?" she goes, seeing as I wasn't going to give her any more clues. "He's out," I said, "I don't know when he will be back." That was perfectly true. I never do know when he'll come back. I've never known anyone with such a talent for being side-tracked. He's all right once he has the coffee in his hand. Then he comes back like a homing pigeon. "Eiow" she says. "Well, I do need to speak to him." "May I ask what about?" I asked. She looked at me as if a bird had just crapped on my head and I hadn't noticed, but then she says airily, as if it's not remotely important to her though I can see that it is, "About that Venice thing," and passes me her card. Honest to God, her name's actually Venetia. I say "I'm sorry, but we only work with people we know." That's when her mouth opened like a sink hole. I half-expected to see a car resting against her epiglottis. I have no idea whether she remembered me specifically, but it was obvious she recognised her own words.'

'You struck a blow for all the people she's said that to. Go, girl!'

'Well, *she* did. She shot out the door so fast that she banged into poor James and spilt our lattes.'

'There are a lot of people like that in the art world in the UK,' said Joe, 'as you've found out. I think it was one of the reasons why I avoided living my dream for as long as I did. Italy is easier that way. History of Art is taught in a lot of state high schools same as any other subject, as an integral part of Italy's cultural patrimony. There should be more jobs in the field than there are, but we're getting there. It's not the preserve of rich kids who can afford gap year courses. But, we still have to soft-soap the rich for sponsorship. Fortunately not all of them are Philistines by a long chalk.'

'What about the people who use art to cover up whatever dirty business they're up to?' asked Juliet.

'Oh, there are plenty of those,' said Joe. 'Not just Russians, though Professor Girotti has turned some of them away. Sometimes you don't know that's what they are. You can launder sponsorship money same as you can launder any other kind. And then there are the big guns. Sackler and their opioid money. Or the oil and gas companies sponsoring museums while destroying the planet.'

'Aren't we doing that too, Joe, with all our cheap flights?'

'There are ways of solving that, Ash, if you want. Just come and live with me. But the both of you have to be there for next month's bash. It's going to be about raising funds. Figgs is invited too, of course.'

It was a beautiful September evening when Joe helped Ash into the motor-taxi that was to take them across to the Giudecca. Ash nearly opened her mouth to say 'It's OK, I can manage,' so used as she was to getting on and off Transport for London's finest without help, but the little old-fashioned gesture went with Joe's appearance. He was wearing what he explained Italians called a *frac,* which to Ash sounded like what you did when you were trying to access gas supplies and didn't care if you produced an earthquake in the process, but which looked like a particularly smart tuxedo. His clothes fitted him sleekly, contrasting with the thickness and increasing length of his dark hair. Byronic, Jules had called him. Ash was only sorry she hadn't said it first.

'You look great,' she said.

'Thank you. It's hired,' he said. 'And this boat will turn into a pumpkin at midnight. You look great too.'

'It's hired too – Juliet's new sideline.' She smoothed the crisp fabric of the 1960s Biba dress. Its long sleeves with buttoned cuffs added a demure touch, and the full skirt a playful edge, but the fitted bodice and v-neck made her look more voluptuous than she usually allowed herself to feel.

Joe's hand stroked lightly down her back. He put his mouth close to her ear so that she could hear him over the thrum of the engine, his breath warm on her skin. 'Where's the zip, Ash? So's I can pull it down later...'

The boat had already rounded the point of the island and was making its way quickly along the shoreline to the villa. Ash could already see the lights amongst the trees. As they reached the landing-stage she could see the first floor terrace was thronged with people, the long windows sparkling with the diffused light of Murano glass chandeliers. As the boat's motor reduced to a hum, she could hear chatter and laughter. She felt anxious, self-doubting, in a way she hadn't for months, but the way she'd once been used to feeling. She remembered that Venetia girl at the New Bond Street gallery, telling her there wouldn't be a job for her as she wasn't one of the 'people we know.' Then she remembered her own put-down, months later, and James laughing about it as he sponged spilt latte off his waistcoat. Joe's presence reassured her; Joe was the person *everyone* knew. And Professor Girotti knew her and had specifically asked that she, and

James Figgs, be there. Ashley was acutely aware that this was a donor event. Pleasing the guests that evening could be crucial to the Institute's future, for the specialist equipment they needed, for the deserving but disadvantaged students they hoped to find sponsorship for. Joe had confirmed that Covid and then the war in Ukraine had battered the Villa's finances, though Recovery Fund finances from Brussels and the unswerving support of the mayor of Venice had kept things going. But Ashley remembered Professor Girotti's steely look when she'd told her of all the Russian funding she had turned away. 'I refuse to provide Putin with any cultural capital,' she'd said, though at the same time she'd championed the presence of the Russian students who'd told her with tears in their eyes that the régime did not speak for them. 'They will build the new Russia someday,' was her answer to anyone who so much raised an eyebrow.

And now, walking up to the villa from the jetty with her hand in Joe's, Ashley realised that of course she did know people. There was Davide with Juliet, invited by Joe, standing with James Figgs. There was Professor Girotti, waiting to welcome them, like the line-up after a wedding. Then she felt Joe's hand tighten. His entire body stiffened. Just behind Professor Girotti's shoulder were the last two people Ash would have expected to see again. The woman was waving, calling Joe's name in a shrill voice.

They were Rupert and Wanda Brant.

Chapter Twenty-three

Villa Hériot, the Giudecca
September 2022

Wanda almost knocked into Professor Girotti in her impatience to get past her. Tottering on spindly heels that made her taller than her husband, in a cloud of silk chiffon in a psychedelic pattern, Wanda launched herself at Joe. He didn't let go of his grip of Ash's hand, even when the woman wrapped herself around him, smearing lipstick first on one cheek, then the other. Apart from the renewed pressure on Ash's hand, Joe stood as firm and unmoving as an oak tree.

'Good evening, Mrs Brant,' he said with distant courtesy, as the woman stood back, her fingers flat to her mouth in an exaggeratedly coquettish gesture, though Ash did wonder if she was really trying to hide the mess she'd made of her lipstick.

'Oh, Joe, no need to be so formal with *me* of all people, is there?' She fished a tissue from her beaded clutch bag and dabbed it at her mouth, before folding it and wetting it with the point of her tongue, without taking her eyes from Joe. She then tried to wipe the scarlet smudges from Joe's cheek, but he jerked his head away.

'Oh, *Joe,*' she said, her head on one side. 'I always did overdo it, didn't I darling?'

'Yes,' said Joe evenly.

'Oh!' said Wanda, 'no need to take on so. Not with a friend as old as I am.'

'You've met my fiancée, I think,' said Joe.

Fiancée? Or perhaps he just means it in the Italian way – fidanzata. Just don't go there, Ash, you've caused enough trouble already.

Wanda turned to her as though she'd only just noticed she was there, something Ash knew was impossible. In a cloud of perfume too expensive for Ash to be able to identify it, despite numerous forays 'up west' with Juliet in search of tester samples, Wanda deigned to air kiss her – 'Mmm! Mmm!'

'Worked in admin, didn't you? Elsie? Aileen?'

You know perfectly well.

'I work for James Figgs the art dealer now.'

'How nice for you...' She turned back to Joe. 'Sweet of *you* to stay in touch with old colleagues,' she told him.

Did I really hear him say fiancée? If he did, she's not heard it? Or was it only wishful thinking?

'Would you excuse us,' said Joe. 'Ashley and I ought to greet our host.'

Wanda tittered and gripped his free arm in a crimson-manicured vice. 'Don't be long! We have *so* much to catch up on!'

'Please excuse us,' said Joe again, shrugging her off. He put his arm around Ash's shoulder and they went forward to where Professor Girotti stood; Ash could feel Joe shaking – with rage or fear? With his colleague he managed to put across an air of calmness, but Ash wasn't fooled. Joe had form, after all, in keeping very quiet about what he was really feeling.

Ash wondered though what Professor Girotti had made of Wanda's gush over Joe, but more than that she wondered what the Brants were doing there – though when she looked around, Rupert Brant had apparently disappeared.

'They're potential donors,' said Juliet. 'Davide did a bit of nosing about.' In a lull in the party, she and Ash were standing on the central terrace, looking across the moonlit water. Below them, on the grass, Joe was in deep conversation with a man she vaguely knew from London, a representative of the British Association of Paintings Conservator-Restorers. A short distance away James Figgs was standing under a tree with an elegant, long-haired man of about forty, but judging by their laughter and the way they leaned into one another, Ash judged the conversation wasn't entirely a professional one.

'But they were never interested in anything like art. Why now? And why *here*?' said Ash.

'I think there's trouble in paradise, is why. I ran into Wanda in the ladies. The light in there isn't exactly flattering, not like moonlight and chandeliers. I suppose they're so used to strong lights for working on paintings that they apply the same principle in the bogs. See all the cracks and flaws so you can zap 'em with Botox or whatever the latest facial Polyfilla is. La Brant didn't recognise me, or pretended she didn't.'

'She did that with me out there with Joe. I'm sure she'd've walked right past me if he hadn't been there. She was practically enamelled to him.'

'I don't think you need to bother your head on his part, Ash. And Wanda looked *terrible*. You can kind of understand it after all that time under lockdown, no chances to travel, but I'd say she'd overdone it with the Bermuda sun. You remember how she used to look as smooth as wax?'

'How could I forget it?'

'Well, her skin's gone all dry and coarse, enlarged pores and everything. Even Crème de la Mer would know when it's beat. I saw creases in her neck when she moved her face from side to side. She's got that much slap on that she could be wearing one of those Pierrot masks you can buy here, only they're made of china and meant for hanging on the wall. And as for her hair, all tonged and piled up like that, it has enough spray on it that you could rap a spoon on it and it'd go tink tink tink. Those accidentally on purpose tendrils look like steel wool.'

'You almost make me feel sorry for her.'

'Well, don't. Even though word is they're divorcing.'

Ash nearly spilled her drink.

'So that's why she was all over Joe. How did she even know he was here?' In the next second, she knew why. Joe featured on Insta, Twitter, Mastodon, Facebook, you name it. Not that he deliberately put himself out there – that wouldn't have been the Joe she knew – but he featured on all the social media channels where Villa Hériot was active. It would have taken a bored and embittered woman looking out on a Bermudian sunset only a couple of minutes to locate him.

'That's the easy bit. It's not like he's Lord Lucan. But you can't be worrying about her and him. Joe adores you.'

Ash watched the flotilla of boats ahead of theirs in the water. She and Joe were travelling back with Davide and Juliet. James Figgs wasn't with them, for when it came to leaving, neither he nor the man he'd been talking to under that tree were to be found anywhere.

It was such a beautiful night that they asked to be put down at Piazza San Marco. As Ash stepped out of the taxi onto the Molo, she realised that this should have been a beautiful moment, walking on a cloudless early autumn night into the place she'd read Napoleon had called 'the drawing-room of Europe.' The man she loved had his arm around her shoulder, the man who had earlier described her to his ex-lover as 'my fiancée.' And with her was her bestie, the person she knew would be there for her no matter what, hand in hand with a handsome Venetian, someone worthy of Jules at last.

Everything should have been perfect and could have been until that moment that Wanda Brant teetered across on her Louboutins, shrieking Joe's name.

The two couples parted on the Molo, Davide leading Juliet along the Riva degli Schiavoni towards his flat in Castello. In near silence, Ashley and Joe walked towards the Campo Santa Maria Formosa by instinct, though there were quicker ways to Joe's flat. In the Campo itself, a few late diners lingered at the tables outside Davide's restaurant. Ash saw a dark figure leaning against the wellhead, with close by a blur of white. The minute Killer picked up their scent, he bounded over, Gianni running after him, before the dog in his enthusiasm had a chance to make a mess out of Joe's hired trousers. The three humans spoke for a few minutes, Joe explaining where they'd been.

'You two have an interesting life, I think,' said Gianni. Ash thought he looked tired and sad, but told herself it was late, and Gianni probably had some pressing work problem.

'Give our best to Donatella,' she said.

When Gianni had gone, Ash said, 'Out with it. There's

something you're not telling me.'

'I'm going to make this come right, Ash, I promise you,' said Joe, after a pause. 'I don't know how, but I will.'

'Go on,' Ash said, feeling as though her heart was beating in her throat.

'I'm being blackmailed, in a way. I don't know how else to describe it.'

Ash stopped dead. 'What, actual blackmail? For money?' She had visions of photos of a naked Joe, *her* naked Joe, in the clutches of Wanda Brant. She thought she'd suffocate, imagining those bony feet in their red soled shoes rocking on Joe's broad shoulders.

'No, moral blackmail I suppose you'd call it. But everything is at risk – everything but us, that is, at least I hope – I mean me getting to stay at the Villa Hériot.'

'No! But they adore you! Professor Girotti—'

'Funds not adding up is the problem. The Brants are offering sponsorship, about half a million euros of it. There's also a painting she wants to give to the institute. She said it's by Giorgio somebody-or-other, but she couldn't remember the name. She said the painting could be auctioned. Rupert must have had more funds offshored than he ever told *me* about. It even crossed my mind that he could still do me harm as an accountant – not that I intend going on being one, but I have to stay chartered if I'm to do odd jobs like keeping Figgs's books in order. I mean, if there is ever any investigation into his business, I know *I've* done nothing wrong but the attention wouldn't do me much good.'

'Can't you just ride that out? As you said, accountancy isn't your future anyway.' But as she said it, Ash knew worse was coming.

'That half a million would make a huge difference. There are three young conservators, for instance, from the centre in Kyiv-Pechersk, that Professor Girotti wanted to bring here. The Russian invasion has upended their lives. Brant money would enable them to finish their training – and plenty of other things besides.'

'Why are the Brants interested in Villa Hériot?' asked Ash, wishing there wasn't such a tremor in her voice. 'I don't remember them being into art patronage before. Sport, yes. Theatres sometimes. But never sums like that. And Juliet had heard they were divorcing. She picked that up from Davide of all people. I don't know how.'

'They were eating at his restaurant the other day. They were talking about the institute and their own separate plans. Davide told Juliet there'd been an English couple who didn't care how much of their dirty laundry he heard about. He remembers them because they behaved as if he wasn't there, as if he didn't count. The way people in big houses used to behave in front of the servants – my great-grandmother told me that – she was in service in Ireland when she was thirteen. When the Brants stepped off the boat at Villa Hériot he recognised them straightaway, but of course they didn't recognise him. I think they see themselves as some kind of Bill and Melinda Gates. Yes, they've split up but they want to make out they are so civilised that they don't let that get in the way of being benefactors. It's all a sort of whitewashing or greenwashing or whatever it's called – making them look nobler than they really are. But of course the Ukrainian conservators will just be grateful to be helped. I don't know if you knew, but Wanda is partly Russian, in a Helen Mirren sort of way, through her father, but she's been brought up as English. The future Mrs Brant is however Russian to the core.'

'How do you know this?'

Joe sighed. 'Hold me, Ashley.'

She did so, feeling the pounding of his heart through his shirt. There was something else about him, though, less tangible. It was almost as if he gave off a scent, nothing that she could identify other than to say that it was there. Instinct told her it was fear.

'I know because Wanda came up and told me, the minute the man from BAPCR went to talk to someone else. She said the woman even looked pretty much like her, only twenty years younger. I know I should have felt sorry for her or should have said something flippant like "congratulations on your lucky escape" but all I wanted was to get away from her. The scholarship scheme is part of the deal for a civilised divorce. Wanda's been mugging up on the arts scene, but honest to God, to hear her, you'd think she'd bought one of those bluff your way in whatever-it-is books you can buy in airports. Ash, it's a classic rebound. She thinks she can have me.'

'Joe!'

'She said... oh dear... she said she'd never had such a good lover.' Joe recounted the compliment in a shaking voice.

Ash pulled away. 'I think I'm going to be sick.'

He grasped her shoulders. 'She can't have me. She just can't. I wouldn't be physically capable of going anywhere near her now. Even the smell of her perfume makes me want to gag. But she's gone and told Professor Girotti that she and Rupert Brant want to fund the scholarships because of *me*. God help me, but Professor Girotti was so grateful to me. She thinks I deliberately brought the Brants to the institute. What am I going to tell her?'

'There has to be a way out of this, Joe,' said Ash. 'I have no idea what it is, but we'll have to find it. Let's go home, Joe, pick up Hetty, shower the evening off ourselves. I don't think you should tell Professor Girotti what's behind this, or not yet. Let's not put her in an awkward position. But can I tell Juliet?'

'I'd expect you to.'

'And James Figgs?'

Joe hesitated. 'Why him?'

'Partly because he knows this world so well. He knows all the players. Not just who has slept with who, but where grants are to be had. Something to replace this half a million euros.' But Ash felt breathless even naming that figure. 'Because I trust him. And also —'

'Go on.'

'Because I haven't a clue what to do. I just feel I want to blurt to someone, that's all.' And Ash burst into tears as Joe's arms went around her.

'Ash, Ash,' said Joe, into her hair. 'I don't know either. Do you think you could settle for a boring accountant after all?'

'I'd settle for you any day, whatever you did for a living,' she said, her voice muffled in his shirt front.

'Oh hell, what's this now?' she heard him mutter, distracted. Somewhere close by there was a splatter of sound, too loud for the square at that time of night. Even before she could make out the words, from the cadence of their voices she knew they were English, Londoners mostly by the sound of them, and they weren't sober.

'Hey, you!' someone shouted. Ash felt Joe's arms stiffen around her.

'Get her home and get her fucked, mate, or I'll do it for you!' continued the voice.

Ash thought she had to be hallucinating. *First the Brants. Now — no it couldn't be!*

'I'm not having that,' muttered Joe, easing her away, and turning to face the group of revellers. Ash thought there were six of them, but Joe stood between her and them so she couldn't see every face. 'Which one of you bastards said that?' shouted Joe.

'Joe, don't. Joe—' She tugged his arm.

One of the group stepped forward. 'I don't know who the hell you are,' he said, his eyes struggling to focus on Joe, 'but I know you've no business kissing my girlfriend.'

'*What?*'

'Deaf, are you? Or just foreign?' said Ed.

Joe launched himself at Ed, not punching but pushing. Ed staggered, but his companions broke his fall. He shoved them away and made to rush at Joe, but hands clutched at him, though one of them shouted, 'No, are you going to let him get away with it?' gesturing at Joe. Another man put a hand on Joe's shoulder. 'Leave it, mate? Though maybe the lady has some explaining to do.'

Ash found her voice at last.

'I have *no* explaining to do. That man is not my boyfriend,' she added firmly, pointing at Ed, 'And I'm the one who decides who gets to kiss me, not him. So clear off, the lot of you.'

'But he assaulted me!' whined Ed, trying to free himself. Seconds later, his companions let go in disgust, for Ed opened his eyes wide, his body convulsed, and he was promptly sick over his own feet.

'Let's get out of here, Ash,' said Joe.

Chapter Twenty-four

Cannaregio

Hetty was waiting behind the door to greet them. Ash scooped her up, and laid her face against warm, vibrating fur. Joe closed the door quietly and put his arms around them both.

'I had no idea he was going to be here,' she said for at least the third time since they'd run from the Campo.

'I know,' Joe said patiently. 'But what I don't know is *why* he's here.'

Ash shrugged. 'A stag night? For all I know it might be his.'

'They didn't look quite like stags to me,' said Joe. 'Not that I've been to hundreds – just with a couple of cousins in Ireland. That polo shirt and chinos look says business casual to me. They'll be at a trade show or something.'

'I never told you, did I? He said he was going to propose to me here.'

'Oh, he did, did he? In a gondola, I suppose.'

'Actually, yes.'

Joe muttered something Ash couldn't quite catch, though she thought she heard 'rules that out then.'

'You're being blackmailed by Wanda Brant and Ed has turned up again. It can't get any worse, can it, Joe?'

'Nope – unless you decide you don't like me after all.'

'Oh, Joe!' Hetty tactfully jumped out of her arms and Joe bent to kiss her.

'It seems like an age ago when we put these on, doesn't it?' said Ash, turning so that Joe could pull down her zip. The dress fell to the floor with a hiss and a sigh. The *frac* was hanging from the wardrobe door on the hire company's hanger. As Joe unbuttoned his shirt Ash ran her fingers down his chest. Later, they huddled together in bed not for warmth but for reassurance.

'We have this,' Joe murmured as he dipped his head to kiss her.

'Can I?' he added after the kiss ended. In answer, Ash pulled him over her and her legs opened as if of their own accord.

'Always,' she whispered.

The next day matched their mood: a glowering sky and at last the release of a thunderstorm. Hetty hid in a cupboard, mewing pathetically. Ash took her food to her and tried to reassure the little animal. She had slept badly, her mind going round and round in circles. Surely Professor Girotti would understand… Joe had made it clear that Wanda was not going to have things her way. 'I physically couldn't do it with her again, Ash,' he'd said for the nth time, staring up at the dark ceiling at one a.m.

'Would you, if there hadn't been me?'

There was a long silence. 'It's an unfair question, Ash. You *are* there – thank God. Would I have tried, to save Villa Hériot? Fuck knows.'

He'd got up then and gone to the kitchen for a glass of water, but being Joe, came back carrying one for her. Ash watched the pale shimmer of his body in the gloom and felt an unaccustomed twinge of jealousy. *Wanda doesn't really want him – only she wants to know she can have him* if *she feels like it.*

In the morning Ash zoomed with James Figgs. The background didn't look like a hotel-room. There were shelves of art books, for a start. She decided to get to the point as soon as possible.

'Whatever are you calling me for, Ashley? I thought you were meant to be in the arms of the estimable Joe.'

'Oh James. I just don't know where to start.'

'At the beginning usually works best. Out with it. You look as if you haven't slept.'

'I haven't. Not much.'

'Is Joe with you?'

'He's gone to the Giudecca. But just for the morning. He

knows I want to speak to you. He and I are fine – absolutely fine – other people are the problem. Well, one in particular.'

'That botoxed harpie with the mouth like a blow-up beach toy, I expect.'

'Wanda Brant. How did *you* know?'

'Thought I was too engrossed in that elegant journalist to notice? Oops. Ought to keep my voice down. He's not just elegant but extremely hospitable with it. I do rather like this flat of his. How did I know? Put it down to an old auctioneer's perspicacity. My ability to spot the smallest signals from a distance – not that that was needed in the case of La Brant. She was pretty bloody obvious – hands on arms, brushing herself against people and showing her teeth with all the charm of an insect-eating plant. She made a pass at Renzo – that's the elegant journalist – enough to force him to tell her he wasn't in the vagina business, after which she became embarrassingly fawning. We could both see she wanted your chap but that he definitely didn't want her.'

'She's already had him,' said Ash miserably.

'Oh, poor show,' said Figgs. 'I expect he was put up to it.'

'Sort of. The problem is that she wants him back so she's trying to blackmail him.'

'Got pictures, has she? That kind of thing has a habit of rebounding. And anyway, Joe's told you, so she hasn't got any hold of him anymore.'

'It's to do with the institute,' said Ash, and told him the entire story.

'I see,' said James eventually. 'Give me a couple of days, if you would. Baldrick has the glimmerings of a cunning plan. Might I discuss this with the elegant journalist?'

'Of course. If you trust him.'

'I do. I shan't tell anyone else – yet. But bear in mind that the last thing a blackmailer wants is publicity. Their whole objective is to sell their silence. Miss Rubber-lips is playing a variation on that theme. I think there is a way to turn the tables, without your Joe needing to shed a single garment – do forgive the mixed metaphors. In the meantime, you are not to worry, though I expect you will. Tell Joe he needn't either. He shouldn't spill the beans to Professor Girotti just yet – but he will be able to, once the institute has the woman's money. Because they will get it. Only, I have a suggestion to make, Ashley, though you may not care for it.'

'Which is?'

'I think Joe should go along with her.'

'No!'

'Only to give us enough time to plot. I'm not suggesting that he knows the woman carnally again. He could play the wounded genius for a bit. You know, "There is nothing I would like better, but I am no use to womankind at present" sort of thing.'

'He won't like it.'

'See if he can find out more about that painting she's offering too. I expect it's some terrible old daub, if as you say she knows nothing about art, but you never know.'

'He was completely unfazed, Joe. It was as if he's dealt with things like that many times before. He made Wanda sound like an amateur, out of her depth.'

'I'm really not sure about his suggestion I go along with her. I can't stand being around the woman. Not that I could do anything with her.'

'I know that. But just to be arm candy for a bit while we all figure out what to do. There's that painting she mentioned. But how did you get on this morning? You've not told Professor Girotti, have you?'

'Look, I'll think about it. No, I've not told Cecilia though there were many times I thought, "Just spit it out, Joe, and get it over with." She knew something was wrong, right enough. You can't do the kind of work we do without someone who knows you well noticing. It's to do with the level of concentration. But she did this marvellous thing, Ash. Not one conservator in a hundred would have done it. I'd been working on a canvas by Palma Giovane. There must be work by him in just about every church in Venice. You'll have seen them even if you didn't know they were his. You could almost call him an interior decorator. He has a kind of bravura, I suppose, and he was good at portraiture. I shouldn't be critical as I'm not much of an artist and he did have an admirable work ethic.'

'You *are* a good artist.'

'You mightn't say that if I tried a portrait of you. But thank you for the vote of confidence. Anyway, I struggled for an hour at dabbing away the candle smoke from this crucifixion, but I just couldn't settle and Professor Girotti saw it. She told me to leave off and I thought I was going to get a talking to. Instead she showed me a new work that had come in. Ash, it's potentially a beautiful thing, but so compromised. It's a small panel painting by Alvise Vivarini of the Virgin and Child. It was in a private collection on Murano, where Vivarini came from – a family heirloom – but now there's nobody left to inherit. There's worm in the wood, and the faces were repainted, probably in the seventeenth century by the look of them, also because it's in a horribly ornate frame from that time. Various specialists will have to work on it but I am to be lead conservator. That's a hell of a responsibility – especially to get it so early in my career.'

'Because she trusts you,' said Ash.

'She does. Am I going to blow that trust?'

'Not with the painting, you're not.'

'I have to prove her right. Anyone else would have sent me home to sort myself out, which would have meant I'd have been sitting here mentally beating myself up. Instead she gave me a greater responsibility, one she knew I could lose myself in. I did too. While I was doing the initial examination, organising the first tests we do, Wanda bloody Brant never crossed my mind. What is it, Ash?'

'Nothing probably. You know Professor Girotti better than I do. Do you think it's possible that she gave you the work because you were going to get all this money for the institute?'

Joe hesitated. 'Oh hell ... You know what? I don't think so. It's really not the way she works. She told me she'd had more than one application for a place where the student's father was a rich industrialist prepared to make a significant donation if their kid was accepted.'

'Bribes, you mean?'

'Yeah, that's the word she used. She knocked them back – said they were nearly all spoiled rich kids their parents didn't know what to do with. All except one where the girl concerned really did have some talent. Professor Girotti gave her even more of a grilling than an applicant would normally get. It turned out that the father – a New York realtor - wanted his daughter to be a lawyer or a banker or something. The girl had fought hard for what she wanted, until eventually the father gave in. Threatened to go to Europe to work in a shop until she could fund her own way.'

'Sounds like St Ursula in that painting, counting off on her fingers her conditions for marrying the prince.'

'It does, doesn't it? Anyway, the girl is in her second year now and doing really well. But Professor Girotti has agreed with her father in writing that no donation will be made until after the girl has done her final exams, and if she doesn't do well, or even doesn't get the top marks he thinks are her due, he is under no obligation to make it. It's not failsafe, I know, because you could argue that there's strong pressure on to give her top marks, but there is a risk involved. The point is, that student got in on merit and Professor Girotti didn't want to discriminate against her just because she's rich. To be fair, Vanessa doesn't act as if she is. She's in lodgings. Her father bought an apartment in the Dorsoduro thinking to put her in there. She refused even to go and see it.'

'I think you could come clean with Professor Girotti.'

'I do too. I won't only because Figgs says not to just yet. Hey, Ash. I'm not due back at the institute until tomorrow, but I need to walk off my restlessness a bit. What if I get us Chorus tickets and after lunch we go and see some churches?'

'Chorus?'

'Nope, not singing. It's a volunteer organisation. They keep open about fifteen of the churches in Venice that would otherwise be closed apart from when they are saying Mass in them – *if* they are still saying Mass in them. San Giovanni in Bragora is one. It's where Antonio Vivaldi was baptised, really quickly because he wasn't that strong a baby, apparently. They've got three paintings by Alvise there and they are really representative of his career. You can see the influence of Giovanni Bellini in one, Antonello da Messina in another one, Andrea Mantegna in the third one — why are you looking at me like that?'

'Because you're on a roll, Joe, and I love you for it. Only

not fifteen churches in an afternoon, maybe. And perhaps not Santa Maria Formosa. Not before we're sure Ed's work thing is well over and he's gone home.'

'We can get to San Giovanni Bragora another way just to make sure. And no, not all the churches in one go. The tickets last a year. So when you come back ... You will come back?'

'If you'll have me. I'll be back next month for Gianni and Donatella's big day, remember?'

'Oh yes. And of course I'll still have you. That's if I am still here.'

'You will be, Joe. You'll need a lifetime to see everything that's here in this city.'

'I want that lifetime. And I want you in it. You wouldn't get bored doing those things with me?'

'I wouldn't, Joe.'

Two nights later it was Hetty who woke first. Ash turned in the bed, to see the little cat silhouetted against the first light of dawn. Joe had got into the habit of leaving one shutter open, so that he would wake naturally with the dawn, instead of by a ring tone. Thanks to the war in Ukraine, lighting across the city had been reduced, a decision that lent greater mystery to the alleyways and quiet night-time canals.

Ash went still. Someone outside was scuffling. She wondered if it was the rubbish collection, but usually they were super-fast, gathering up the bags and slinging them straight into a boat, and anyway, this wasn't their collection day. It was too early for the postman. Nobody had any real reason to lurk below the flat, as the shop that used to be there looked as though it had been shuttered up for a long time. The most she ever heard were people walking briskly past.

She glanced over her shoulder at Joe, sleeping soundly, his solidity a defence against the world, she thought.

Horribly, suddenly, whoever was out there burst into an offkey, unaccompanied attempt at 'O Sole Mio.'

Joe stirred. Hetty bristled and made a strange chattering sound, like the bark of a squirrel.

Omigod! He's singing in English!

'You were my girl once, the only girl for me yeah
We were meant for each other and you know it
But you think I'm not good enough for you now...'

Here the singing was interrupted by a loud belch. By now Joe was awake and pulling on his trousers.

'Stay down, Ash,' he said. 'Don't let him see you,' for she was swinging out of bed and heading for the window.

'You were my girl once, the only girl for me yeah
I'll teach you a lesson, you and him a lesson
O sole mio you are a bitch'

'How did he know where to come?' she cried.

'He must have followed us the other night. Or more likely, that sidekick of his. Ed looked too drunk to find his own shoelaces.'

*'O sole, o sole mio, what are you doing
Up there with him?'*

'Can't we just pretend we're not here?'

'Nope. That's downstairs opening their shutters. He'll wake the whole neighbourhood. Obviously didn't get the #EnjoyRespectVenezia memo. I'm going to deal with him.'

'Joe!'

But he was gone. Ash heard the slam of the flat door and a moment later, the street door opening. She crept to the window to listen.

'Well, look who's here! You even *smell* of her, you bastard!'

'Get lost now, mate, or it's the police,' rumbled Joe. Ash marvelled at how calm he was. 'You can have the local ones, two canals away, or the carabinieri, who can get here in five minutes. If you weren't so stocious, I'd just shove you in that water there and have done with it. Only I like this place. I don't want it polluted.'

'Not goin' anywhere! Want Ash. She's mine!'

'Keep your voice down.'

'O sole mio!'

'Shut up!'

'Pity about the fuckin' gondola.'

'*What* gondola?'

'Lost my way, didn't I? Navigator wasn't working and then my phone fell in the friggin' water. Bloody thing wouldn't steer right anyway.'

'You took a gondola?' Ash could hear Joe's incredulity. 'It takes about four hundred hours of practice to get a license to scull one of those things. And it's a man's living – like stealing his lorry. I *am* phoning the police. That's if they're not looking for you already. Theft *and* causing a public nuisance. Nice one, Ed.'

'S'all your bloody fault. If you hadn't stolen my girlfriend—'

'Catch yourself on, you pure eejit. You can't steal a woman the way you can steal a car – or a gondola in your case. She lives and breathes and makes her own choices. Have sense, would ye? She left you – I know that's hard – and I came on the scene long afterwards. Move on from it. All you're getting from this is a criminal record. You'll probably lose your job too.'

Ash stood by the window but behind a shutter, mindful of Joe's advice not to be seen. She was holding Hetty, trying not to squeeze the little animal too tight from nerves. The voices stopped then, replaced by a series of grunts and the sound of scuffling feet. She knew they were grappling with each other down there. Joe was strong, but she knew violence wouldn't come easily to him. Whereas Ed was not just lubricated with drink and spoiling for a fight but presumably had kept up his bench-presses.

She heard an exasperated neighbour on the floor below fling back her shutters and yell, '*Basta! Inglesi di merda!*' Ash agreed wholeheartedly. It *was* enough, and shit was the right way to describe Englishmen fighting before breakfast-time on a quiet canal. Ed was muttering now, whilst gasping for breath. Ash couldn't make out many words, but the ones she could hear were offensive enough and could only have been applied to her. The next sound was an inarticulate cry of rage she recognised as Joe's, followed by running feet.

Ash let Hetty jump out of her arms and looked out of the window, to see two blurry shapes disappearing over the nearest bridge. From what she could make out, it was Joe doing the chasing.

'Leave him, he's not worth it!' she cried, for nobody to hear.

Ash thought wildly about running after them, but she wasn't even dressed. *It might only make things worse. And I'm afraid of meeting the neighbours on the stairs. What on earth could I say to them?* They were kind people who liked Joe, and were always ready to cat-sit whenever he went to London. The only thing she could think to do that was constructive was to have a cup of tea. She put the water to boil and reached into the cupboard, not for her own green tea, but the box of Barry's tea that Joe had brought back from his last trip to Ireland; he'd told her the taste of it reminded him of summer holidays at his grandmother's.

Ash went to sit on the tousled bed. Joe's pillow still carried the indent of his head and the bottom sheet still held his warmth. She bent over and pressed her face against it. Venice was starting to wake up. There was a rumble of a barge in the canal below, the tread of feet, but none of them recognisable as Joe's. She wished Juliet hadn't gone back to London the day after the party, but as she'd said she couldn't leave *Lucia* for long. It was going to be too early to speak to her, wasn't it?

It wasn't. Juliet answered the WhatsApp call straightaway. The phone was propped against something in the Lucia backshop – probably a sewing-machine.

'Sorry it's so early,' began Ash.

'Phwass happtnt?' said Juliet, her mouth full of pins. Ash saw her lean forward to drop the pins into her palm.

'That's better. Now why are you speaking to me instead of doing delightfully rude things with Joe Mannion's body?'

'Ed's here!' wailed Ash.

'Oh fuck. Not in the flat with you?'

'No. He turned up drunk in the middle of the night and Joe's chased him off. Only there's no sign of Joe coming back.'

'Tell me from the beginning, Ash.'

Eventually Juliet said, 'This is my fault. You're all over *Lucia*'s Facebook page. Everything from our New Jolly haircuts onwards. And he's probably still a friend on my private page. I never thought to remove him.'

'Not your fault. Why shouldn't you show your friends – and customers – what you and me have been up to?'

'Someday I hope we'll both laugh about this. But Ed's not really the problem. Right now it's himself he's messing up. Joe's probably holding onto him while he pukes his soul into a canal, to stop him falling in. It's James Figgs and his cunning plan is the one to watch, but I'm of the view Joe should tell his Professor Girotti the lot in the meantime. I'm not sure she'd want to find out later, even if everything works out just fine.'

'If ... Oh, there's someone at the street door. People coming up the stairs. Men.' Ash moved towards the door of the flat. 'No, not him. They're speaking Italian. Where *is* Joe?'

The key turned in the lock.

'*Joe!* I'll call you back, Jules.'

Chapter Twenty-five

Carabinieri

Ignoring the two men in uniform that stood behind Joe, Ash threw her arms around him.

'You're all wet!'

'I'm all right. All I need is a shower and clean clothes. These two fellas brought me back.' He turned. '*Volete un caffé?*'

'*Sì, grazie. Volontieri.*'

'I'll make it,' said Ash. '*Accomodatevi,*' she added, gesturing at the sofa. In smart dark blue with red piping and gleaming boots, the *carabinieri* made quite a contrast with the sodden Joe. *They didn't pull him out of the water then. He must have got out himself.* As the two sat down, she noticed that what she'd thought were batons on their hips were actually firearms. She went to the kitchen and with trembling hands prepared the caffetiere. *This is surreal.*

She came back with the coffee cups rattling on a tray from nerves. To her relief, Joe reappeared quickly, dressed but rubbing his hair with a towel. He brought the coffee from the stove, pouring it with a steady hand. The younger of the two policemen drained his espresso at one go and getting out a mini recorder, said in almost accent-free English, '*Signorina,* please tell us what happened here this morning.'

'I only heard what happened. I didn't look, except when Joe – Mr Mannion – and Ed ran off,' she began. 'Joe thought it was better Ed didn't see me.'

The policeman nodded encouragingly. Looking at her hands, Ash told as much as she remembered, as Joe sat silently next to her.

'*Micio!*'

Her head shot up. *Micio must mean Puss, or something like it.* The other policeman was succumbing to Hetty on a charm offensive. Ash started to relax. Joe was back. The police obviously just wanted Joe's story corroborated. *Surely they wouldn't be sitting there calmly drinking Joe's coffee and stroking Hetty if he was in trouble?*

She glanced at Joe's profile and then back at the policemen.

'Why was Joe all wet?' she asked.

The younger one smiled. 'Because he is a hero,' he said. 'Thank you for the coffee. We will leave you in peace.' He switched off the recorder and got to his feet.

'What happened, Joe?'

'I lost my temper. Ed called you a tart and some other stuff so I saw red and took a swing at him. He ran off and I went after him. Only because it was still pretty dark, and he kept turning round and giving me dog's abuse, he ran down an alley that was a dead end. Only a dead end in Venice usually involves water. Honest to God, it all seemed to happen in slow motion, watching him falling in. It was like being in a dream, where you just can't move even though you want to. He came up, wet as an otter but flailing, and went straight back down again. So I went in after him. He was in such a bad way that he actually fought me in the water. But I got him to the steps and by then there were four or five people, and they dragged us up onto dry land. While we were both standing there and gasping, hands on knees, the police materialised. Someone must have called them. I thought we were both going to be arrested, as there's probably a law about not swimming in the canals – same as there is about surfboarding – you'll remember those Americans who got arrested for it. Fortunately all the bystanders started talking at once about how Ed had fallen in on his own and I'd rescued him.'

'So where is he now?'

'In clink. I'm not proud of myself. Ed couldn't understand any word of what I said to the police apart from gondola, probably. He'd sobered up after his wetting, though; there was no more shouting out of him either. That was it – they arrested him. Those two officers who brought me back told me a gondola had been found drifting. They were grateful for a quick clear-up, I think. But I did tell Ed I'd contact the honorary consul for him. Not that he thanked me.'

'He wouldn't. What a halfwit. God, Joe, what if there'd never been Covid? I might still be with him.'

'Ssh, Ash,' he said, taking her in his arms. 'It's OK.'

'I'm just off the phone to the British Consulate in Milan,' he said later. 'They've got all the details and will pass it on to their local representative. The woman was a bit starchy but I'm quite sure she was trying not to laugh when I told her about the gondola.'

'And about O *Sole Mio*?'

He paused. 'I never mentioned that. I told the police I didn't want to press charges. Do you mind that? I know I should have asked you first.'

'No, not at all. Oh Joe, all we wanted was a quiet life.'

'That's what I was thinking. I didn't want the plods back here, even if one of them did fall in love with Hetty. I just want to be able to love you without any bother – and of course I'm relieved that there weren't any charges against me. I chased him after all, and I was lucky there wasn't somebody who claimed I pushed Ed in the drink. Or him, for that matter.'

'But you didn't!'

'I feckin' well thought about it, though. When he called you names.'

'What names?'

'It doesn't matter. I've forgotten them.'

'You're a terrible liar, Joe.'

'Good. What I haven't forgotten is what I'd intended to do this morning if we hadn't been so rudely awakened. I should go to the Giudecca this afternoon, but do you think …?

'What'll happen to Ed?' asked Ash later, turning to face Joe's profile on his pillow. 'I mean, it's not that I'm that bothered, but …'

'But you wouldn't want him coming back. Me neither. He'll probably get a hefty fine and be sent home. It might depend on whether there's any damage to the gondola. He'll perhaps have to pay some kind of reparation to the gondoliere for loss of earnings for the time it spends with forensics being dusted for fingerprints. Those guys can earn around a hundred and fifty thousand euro a year and they'll be trying to make back what they lost under Covid.'

'Will you need to give evidence?'

Joe propped himself up on his elbow. 'Maybe, if only to confirm that he told me he nicked it. But if his paws are all over it and there's any webcam evidence then there mightn't be any need. If he's any sense he'll just cooperate and plead guilty. I sort of got the impression from the woman in Milan that they're usually called on for people doing completely silly things. Tourists get fined for lack of respect, mainly. Or for drunkenness. Sunning themselves in swimsuits on the steps of a church, sort of thing. None of them would dream of doing that in front of St Paul's, drunk or sober, would they?'

'He'll lose his job.'

'The look on your face, you'd think it was your fault.'

'Well, if it hadn't been for me —'

'Ash! This is *his* fault. If it's any comfort, even if he does lose his job, if he's as essential to them as you said he'd made out to you he was, they'll contract work out to him. I saw that happen so many times in Gulliver and Brant. Rupert was only bothered about being *seen* to do the right thing. He didn't bother his head about *what* he was actually doing. Hey, talking of the Brants, I don't want to, but I think I'd better get over to the institute.'

'Liar. You *do* want to go.'

'Only because I get to come back to you. Just don't answer the door to any strange men while I'm out.' He leaned over to kiss her. 'It's Ed that's the liar.'

'Oh?'

'Apart from calling you a tart, which you're not, he said you were crap in bed. Well, I know that's not true either. Not remotely.'

'I think it was,' said Ash. 'I don't think we were very good that way. Well, it wasn't very good for me. He didn't behave like he cared, either way. But *you* care, Joe. That makes all the difference.'

'Ash,' he murmured, kissing her again. 'I love you. And you're the sexiest woman alive.'

Joe saw something was amiss the moment he saw Professor Girotti's tense face. She did not even greet him.

'Have you a moment?' she said. 'We could talk in the garden.'

'Of course,' he said, his heart sinking. Professor Girotti swept up her tablet and without a word set off down the wide staircase. He followed her outside, as she looked for a marble bench in the shade. This was something Joe hadn't quite got used to yet. In England – not to mention Ireland – everyone went looking for that sliver of sunshine whenever it appeared. Here in Italy, it was the shade that was prized. *Normal, if you're spoiled with that much sun.* He looked around the quiet garden, remembering the lights of the party, Ash's happy face, their friends. The joy – until the Brants appeared.

Professor Girotti sat, swiping at her screen. After a moment's hesitation, Joe sat beside her.

'I thought this was confidential,' she said, showing him the Venezia Today news site. Joe looked, and his heart sank further. There was Wanda Brant, photographed in a bikini on a sun lounger by the pool of a faux middle-eastern style luxury hotel.

'Where is this?' he muttered.

'The Excelsior on the Lido. Not that it matters,' said

Professor Girotti, irritated. 'Read it, will you?'

Joe read.

> Having heard the rumours that Wanda
> Brant, philanthropist and patron of
> the arts, was considering a major
> donation to a Venetian fine arts
> institution, we decided to catch up
> with her at her hotel on the Lido. Mrs
> Brant was able to confirm that she is
> looking for projects that would help
> young people play their part in the
> cultural rebuild post-Covid.

Glancing references were made to existing foundations, Venice in Peril, Save Venice and others. Joe had to admit that the copy was quite flattering, though there was a complete absence of any reference to any specific art or artists. Joe was pretty sure Wanda would think Alvise Vivarini was a dry white wine, or played in defence for Udinese. But here she was, saying she wanted to do something a bit different from what these other organisations were doing, apparently telling the journalist that where they started with artefacts, she started with people, quoting the proverb about teaching a man to fish instead of just going to the market and buying him one. *That's probably the only thing she's said that she knew already without having to mug it up.*

'She wouldn't have known to say most of those things,'

said Joe. 'Either she's well-briefed or the journalist made it up.'

'There's more, Joe.' She scrolled down, handing the phone to him wordlessly.

> As a mark of her appreciation for the work of the Institute, Mrs Brant has also signalled her intention to donate to them a painting of considerable value, a lost work of Giorgione, no less.

'That'll be worth about fifty million at least,' said Joe. He felt light-headed, slightly nauseous.

'This is much bigger than the sponsorship, Joe. What I don't understand is why *Venezia Today*? It isn't the obvious place to splash news like this. These things need to be curated properly. *Arte Magazine,* yes. *The Art Quarterly.* These people are paparazzi, Joe. How did they know?'

'Honest to God, I didn't tell them,' said Joe, truthfully.

'But you know something about who did, I think. You've not been right since that party, Joe, though I can't fault your work. What's going on? You even look as if you've had a rough night.'

'I did have. Only nothing to do with this.'

Unable to look her in the eye, Joe spilled the beans. And because he couldn't separate one misfortune from another in his own head, he told his colleague about Ed's reappearance and the stolen gondola.

'Please don't blame Ash for telling her boss,' he said. 'She was so unhappy and she wanted to confide in someone. So this might be Figgs's doing, but from the best of intentions.'

Professor Girotti's hand stole over his and squeezed.

'I wish you'd been able to confide in me, Joe,' she said. 'This horrible woman. We don't need to take what she's offering.'

'A Giorgione? You're joking. The Ukrainians—'

'Not at that price. Not a *lux prima noctis.*'

'*Droit de seigneur*? Medieval first night rights?'

'Funny how neither of our languages has a phrase for it, isn't it?' said the professor. 'Yes, I think this article is Figgs's doing, though it's quite possible that Wanda Brant contacted *Venezia Today* herself. That meeting on the sun lounger looks quite set up. I mean, she has make-up on and there are no signs of greasy just-applied sun lotion. She wouldn't know about which art journals to contact, only an on-line click bait site. Wanda looks as though she's enjoying the attention. I bet you we'll find this shared all over her social media sites. So she'll hardly be able to back out, will she?'

'Figgs's cunning plan?'

'I think so. He could teach our publicity people a thing or two, though I think this is Renzo's work. I've known him for years and he's pretty astute. He's clever. I'll admit too I've been a bit of a snob. Does it matter if the money comes from "distinguished" sources?' she asked rhetorically, her fingers tracing quotation marks. 'But we'll not be able to accept the painting, even if – or especially if – it really is a Giorgione. We could never manage the security it would require. I'd prefer it to go to the Accademia, to hang alongside the three they have already.'

'You wouldn't want to sell it and invest the money? The institute would be financially safe for years to come.'

Professor Girotti paused. 'It's tempting. It was the first thing that crossed my mind when I read it was a Giorgione. Mrs Brant might object, to start with. If she didn't, there isn't a guarantee it would stay in Italy. It would probably end up at the Getty, or one of these galleries for whom money is no object. But a Giorgione; it should stay in Venice.'

'*If* it's a Giorgione.'

'Joe, would you do what Ash and Figgs are encouraging you to do? I mean, string her along for a bit.'

'It doesn't feel fair. Not to Ash, and not even to Wanda, even if she gets no more of me than hanging onto my arm.'

'You're too good, Joe. *She* stops at nothing to get what she wants. Only, something doesn't square for me.'

'Nor me. I'm an accountant from Croydon and I'm hardly worth a Giorgione.'

'I am sure Croydon is very nice and being an accountant is no bad thing, except you're now a talented conservator, but yes, it does seem pretty extreme. I mean, when she moves on to someone else, will he get a Picasso?'

'I'm still an accountant and know all about due diligence. We'd need to know the provenance of the painting. Even if it was legitimately acquired, we ought to be wary of why it's being offered to us. We'd want to be sure we're not a front for a money-laundering operation or some other kind of green wash. I had plenty of that with Brant and I can tell you he never liked being stopped. I'd always tell him I'd found out his plans easily, though sometimes I had to dig deep. But it made him jumpy when I told him I'd never had problems catching him out and that made him behave most of the time.'

'If Wanda's divorcing him, then it's in her interests to distance herself from all that, reputationally.'

Joe's phone bleeped. He glanced at it. 'Speak of the devil.'

'Him, or her?'

'Her. She's in Venice. She's asked me to dinner at the Corte Sconta.'

'Are you going to go?'

'If it's all right with Ash, yes.'

'*Forza,* Joe.'

Chapter Twenty-six

The Corte Sconta

'Joe,' purred Wanda, writhing in her seat at the sight of him. Joe resisted the temptation to ask her if she had fleas.

'Quaint place, don't you think?' she said, waving her arm at the steel-framed wicker chairs and plain tables beneath the vine pergola. He was glad though it wasn't an intimate space. The other diners were too noisy for that. He envied them their relaxed laughter, their hands on each other's shoulders.

'I'd heard about this place,' he said. 'Artists and journalists come here.'

'Successful ones, I expect. It's Michelin starred.'

'I wanted to bring Ashley here.'

'Who?' said Wanda in mock surprise. Before he could answer she said, 'You're going to move in different circles now, Joe.'

Despite all his resolution, Joe said, 'I love Ashley.'

'That's your problem,' retorted Wanda, but the toe that

was feeling its way to the skin above his ankle retreated. 'I've ordered for you, by the way.'

Joe lay stretched out on his bed, his shoes kicked off, his eyes shut.

'It was grim, Ash. And it's going to be bloody difficult to navigate and I don't know where to start.'

'Baby steps. Where did you go, first of all?'

'The Corte Sconta. I'd like to tell you what was on the menu, but I can't. Wanda had already chosen for me and I meekly accepted. It was delicious, but that's no excuse for me not being exactly masterful.'

'That's the place Davide wanted to take Jules, only she ended up being a waitress that night at Santa Maria Formosa instead. She had a ball, though.'

Joe took hold of her hand. 'These are the simple, funny things, that happen to people like us and our friends. Not in Wanda-world. At least she played her winning card quickly, only it wasn't so much a winning-card but a two-ton bale of paper dropped on my head. I'll confess to having a drink on the way there to give myself some courage, and Wanda kept the prosecco flowing, though if I'd been one of the waiters I'd have conked her over the head with one of the bottles the way she had them dancing attendance. But when she showed me that photo I felt stone cold sober in an instant.'

'What photo?' asked Ash, thinking of a compromising photo of Joe. *Surely we can get beyond that?*

'The painting. She just had a photo, but it looked convincing. As a Giorgione, I mean. It's a panel painting, about the size of an album cover, if you remember those, of a castle or a walled town. On the grass in the foreground there's a girl, with a unicorn resting its head in her lap. So it's an allegory, just like the painting we know as 'The Tempest', but the meaning is pretty clear. The unicorn in medieval tradition takes shelter in the embrace of a virgin, so what the painting is saying is that chastity is stronger than any fortress. The thing is, Ashley, that there are very few paintings in existence that were certainly painted by Giorgione, maybe only six, though art historians – and dealers – will argue until the cows come home about the attribution of others. When he died of plague he was probably only about thirty-five at most, while his friend Titian was still painting in his late eighties.'

'How did she get hold of it?'

'She was pretty cagey about that. Said it was from a private collection and had just resurfaced. The problem about that is that it could well have been stolen from a Jewish collector who was murdered in the camps, and his family with him. So there might or might not be a relative who could make a claim. The first thing is that I need to see the painting in the flesh.'

'What about Wanda in the flesh?' said Ashley in a small voice.

'Hey, Ash.' Joe sat up and put his arms around her. 'No

danger of that. I told her as much. I don't care what else I'm putting at risk. I'd go back to accountancy to be with you. Here's the funny thing, though. Wanda didn't seem to be bothered that much when I said I wasn't part of the deal. She shrugged and asked me if I'd be interested in seeing other paintings. I asked her who they were by, but she got vague again then and just said she thought they were the kind of things I liked and that we could do business. I don't know why she isn't going to Sotheby's if this is just about selling paintings. Either she didn't want to tell me what else she had, or she isn't interested enough in the artists' names to remember them.'

'It's a puzzle, though. She and Brant are pretty rich but not Abramovich rich. You said a Giorgione would be worth millions.'

Professor Girotti stood on the library steps and rummaged on as shelf two metres from the ground, passing heavy volumes down to Joe. Eventually six of them were spread across a table. The two sat down opposite each other and began their search.

It was Joe who hit lucky.

'This is it – or almost. Not the painting itself but a drawing in red chalk. The background is pretty much the same as the photograph Wanda showed me, but the foreground figure is different. It's a shepherd sitting on a rock, not the maiden with the unicorn resting in her lap. It's a view near

Castelfranco Veneto apparently, but it's been in a museum in Rotterdam for as long as anyone can remember.'

'So the subject is close to where he was born. Let me look up the museum site and see what it says. That book was published in the 1930s so the technical information won't be that up to date.'

Cecilia reached for her tablet. Joe watched her as she tapped on the screen and saw her frown develop.

'The paper is seventeenth century, probably Dutch in origin.'

'So too late and from the wrong place. A forgery, in other words.'

'Or a copy of an original. So Wanda's painting could be a forgery, or a copy too, or an original that this seventeenth-century artist copied. We have to get it into the lab, Joe.'

The painting arrived by speed boat to the landing stage, accompanied by four meaty fellows in too tight suits and wraparound sunglasses. Standing beside Cecilia as they watched its approach, Joe remembered the evening of the party on this very spot, and everyone's surprise at the appearance of the Brants. He could see that the villa's situation on the far side of the island helped the secrecy of the delivery. In the distance he could see a couple of barges moving past the scrubby clump of land that was La Grazia, but that was all.

One of the men stepped off onto the landing stage, then turned back to receive a parcel. He walked towards them along the wooden slats carrying it as though it were a tray and handed it to Joe without a word. The man's expression was impenetrable behind his shades.

'Ashley, you delightful girl! As you see, I am back at the ranch. Cora is in today so I am just about managing in your absence.'

Cora appeared on screen behind Figgs's shoulder.

'Hello Ash!'

'Hello Cora! All good with you and Sally?'

'All good,' said Cora, hugging herself. 'I'll let you two get on,' she said, and disappeared out of view.

'So, Ashley, to what do I owe the pleasure? I am sure you really ought to be in the arms of the Byronic Joe, not phoning some lonely old queen who is trying very hard not to mess things up in your absence.?'

'It's been a bit lively here …'

'Oh do tell!'

'Actually, I was wondering if you could …'

'That jape at the Excelsior, you mean? I thought it came off rather well. You have checked La Brant's social media since?'

'Oh, umm … I hadn't thought to.'

'The woman is basking in her own adoration. I wish I could say it was all my idea, but one needs someone with his ear to the ground, and that was dear Renzo. He knows all the art mag people over there, of course, but he said they all go around looking as if there's a bad smell under their noses and no matter how rich Wanda Woman is they wouldn't be able to disguise the fact they considered her positively *volgare, carissima*! She might be vulgar, but I don't think Wanda is as stupid as she looks. She'd certainly know if she was being made fun of or treated *a sufficienza* as they say where you are. You'll be far too young to remember this, but *I'm* so ancient that I can remember when Victoria Beckham was whatever name she had before she met that delectable fellow with the stubble and the tats. Posh Spice, that's it! The poor dear even deflated her boobs later to look more like a fashion designer whereas everyone thought she looked as if she dressed out of the Littlewoods catalogue no matter how much she'd spent on herself.'

Ash was pretty sure Figgs had never encountered a Littlewoods catalogue in his entire life, suspecting he'd picked up this catty description from somewhere else. Figgs was as usual, irrepressibly entertaining.

'Now of course Mrs Beckham dresses them for the Met Ball, if I'm not mistaken, and all those snobs who wouldn't let her into their clubs back when she was a Spice can't get enough of her. Believe me, dear heart, the art world will come round pretty quickly to Wanda Brant, but Renzo was absolutely right to not aim too high to start with. Have a look at her Insta and you'll see what I mean. She's too late to get her pound of flesh from Joe. Sorry, unfortunate turn of phrase I know.'

'James, there has been a development. Wanda doesn't seem that interested in Joe after all. She's after something else. Could you come here? There's something you ought to see.' She told Figgs the story of the painting.

'Hmm. The drawing in the Netherlands has to be a deliberate forgery or a copy of a lost genuine version. Whatever it is, it's probably not a preliminary sketch for a polychrome painting. Detailed red chalk drawings tend to be works of art in their own right. I shall be on the next flight.' Ashley saw him turn away from the screen. 'Cora! Can you manage without me for a week?'

'I'll see if I can come back home on the same flight as you. I just hope Ed doesn't pull a similar stunt in London, that's all.'

'Might be an idea to change your abode. If he turns up at Figgs's I shall think of something. Probably a combination of Quentin Crisp and George Melly. A high camp recitation of surrealist poetry ought to frighten him off.'

'Oh James!'

'All the more reason for you to decamp to Italy for good, of course. One assumes that Ed, having a criminal record, will not be allowed back in. Though it's never stopped any politicians having their holidays there.'

'But what about my job in the gallery?'

'Precisely. I expect you to work for me in Venice. Cecilia

and I will cook something up between us. Or Cecilia and I and Joe. I think I need an Italian branch.'

Ash sat for some minutes thinking about what Figgs had said about her future. Despite all that had happened, she could not suppress the surge of happiness and hope she felt. Then she sprang into action. First she messaged Joe to say that Figgs was on his way, but decided to keep the possibility of working for Figgs in Venice from him until she was with him in person. It wasn't clear how long that was going to be, as Joe had told her he was going to sleep on a z-bed in the institute for as long as the painting was there. Ashley then googled Wanda Brant. Images of her on the sun lounger at the Excelsior were everywhere. Ash could also see from the woman's pose and expressions that the former trophy wife had been polished until she gleamed and was waiting there in the plate glass window of the world's gaze for the next man who would bid for her. The idea that this man might have been Joe, with his quiet flat, his enjoyment of a vaporetto ride across to the Giudecca instead of going everywhere by speedboat, was just absurd. At least that danger seemed to have receded, but she remembered Figgs saying that she and Joe would probably never be free of Wanda completely, warning of paparazzi following her to the institute. Ash just hoped that the woman would get bored with Villa Hériot, dislike the smell of turpentine, and leave them all alone. The Biennale and perhaps the Guggenheim were more her style.

And as Figgs said, 'Men like Rupert Brant will be about as attractive to her now as warm, flat prosecco. Her job is to find the next rich – much richer – man, to bankroll her in curating the Wanda Brant brand. Seriously, I think we've managed to do the woman a favour. The world? I am not so sure. Relax, dear Ashley. All you have to worry about now are stolen gondolas and drunks singing out of key.'

'Are you disappointed, Professor Girotti?' asked Figgs. He faced her and Joe across the lab bench. László the dendochronologist stood beside him. There had been a moment of excitement when the quiet Slovak had confirmed that the wood was indeed fifteenth century but the mood had deflated when Cecilia and Joe had got to work. The yellowing, cracked varnish which had covered the surface of the painting should have given way to a vibrant blue in the robe of the seated woman and to a vivid green freshness of the grass around her.

'We knew it wasn't quite right when we unwrapped it,' she answered. 'I could see it in all your faces. We all had the same instinct, that the painting was somehow too perfect, but at the same time the girl and the unicorn looked as if they had been pasted on, as if they floated on the grass rather than sat on it and got green stains. Now we have the confirmation. This isn't an old panel hiding behind varnish. It's been painted to look as though it's old. The colours are the same right through.'

'I don't know if you call police,' said László.

'We were offered it,' said Cecilia. 'Wanda did not try to sell us a fake.'

'If we are sure this is fake, then can we look for what is under? Is old panel. Maybe there is old picture there, even if not Giorgione? I x-ray first, of course.'

'Go ahead with the x-ray. But who is going to tell Wanda Brant?'

Everyone shuffled. No one spoke until Joe said, 'I will. Let's finish the job.'

Wanda was already sitting on a red plush banquette in the corner of Caffé Florian. Joe paused in the doorway, watching her preen herself in the multitude of mottled old mirrors that helped lend the place its air of faded rococo glory. She spotted his reflection and waved her red-tipped fingers at him. He sat down opposite her and decided not to point out the smear of grease on her upper lip. The wreckage of Florian's famous little cakes sat before her on a bone china plate.

'I have some bad news, Wanda.'

'Surprise me.'

'The Giorgione is a fake.'

He couldn't contain his surprise when she said, 'Of course it is.'

'You *knew*?'

'I provide work for young artists, Joe. What's left that's genuine these days, Joe?'

Love, he thought.

'Looks like one, doesn't it?' she went on. 'It's like this new AI thing. Just think, you can tell it to write the kind of book you like and it'll do it for you. No need to go looking for stuff that might be disappointing. Find an intelligent art student needing to pay rent and you can have an Old Master of your own. Poor Giorgione didn't live very long either. What my young employees are doing is painting the works he never got a chance to.'

'They're not. The tech might have its place, Wanda, but all it can do is reproduce what is already there. So a painting like that one isn't the development of his craft. It's just a competent copy, but in the process an old work of art, admittedly a humbler one, was painted over. We found a little Madonna and child underneath, probably painted by one of the *madonnieri* producing icons for Venice's Greek community.'

'I remember. It didn't look like much,' she said dismissively.

'You don't really understand anything about art, do you? Look, sell those fakes – they're competent, after all – to the kind of people buying up old country houses or boutique hotels. But tell them what they're getting. It'll keep your young artists in brushes and won't mean they – or you – get arrested for forgery.'

Wanda pouted. 'You really missed an opportunity there, Joe. You could have certified those works and nobody would have been the wiser.'

'I would have been. That's enough for me.'

'Silly man. You'd have got a great cut. But I can see we wouldn't have worked out, would we?'

'Probably not,' croaked Joe, his throat dry. There was something else he had to say but was dreading it. Wanda saved him the trouble.

'Tell the Girotti woman she can keep the half million. I shall go into business selling high end imitations, but my clients would like to see me as a patron of the institute. And besides, my generosity is all over social media. I can hardly take it back now.'

Chapter Twenty-seven

Santa Maria Formosa, October 2022

'What side are we meant to be on?' whispered Ash, as she held Joe's arm walking up the nave of Santa Maria Formosa.

'The groom's side, so the right,' he said. He stood to let her into a pew about five rows from the front. 'I'll just go up and congratulate Gianni. He looks a bit nervous to me.'

As well he might, thought Ash, remembering how only a few metres from where she sat she had inadvertently precipitated Gianni's proposal. She inspected the toes of her silk shoes, dyed to match the rich russet shot-silk of the 1950s style Princess-seamed dress Juliet had managed to magic out of a draggle-tailed long evening dress that Ash hadn't managed to see the possibilities of, much as she loved the fabric. They went rather well with the coral pink and cream of the lozenge-patterned floor. Then she looked around. Gianni, standing to one side of the altar, did indeed look anxious. Davide was alongside him, looking every inch the dependable best man. She couldn't hear what Joe was saying – the little group was too far away and by now the church hummed to the chatter of the two families who were going to be united today – but from his expression she could tell he was being Joe, reassuring, finding the right words.

In front of the altar were what looked like two chairs with very low seats, upholstered in a dashing scarlet trimmed with gold.

But where's Juliet?

'Here I am!' exclaimed Juliet, as though Ash had spoken aloud. In a cloud of Gucci Flora, chandelier ear-rings tinkling, she subsided into the pew beside her friend.

'You look *fabulous!*' cried Ash.

'It works, doesn't it?' said Jules. She twisted in her seat, and the ethereal sprigged muslin of her Ossie Clark dress floated. 'I thought I'd never get here. I'd missed a tiny give in one of the seams and had to fix it.'

'You've worked miracles, Jules.' Ash remembered that dress, hanging up in Juliet's workshop looking mildewed and very sorry for itself, its ivory silk lining ripped beyond repair. Its previous owner had inherited it, finding it before the house clearers came in, but had given it to Jules for nothing, thinking it couldn't be salvaged. Juliet had painstakingly replaced the lining.

The organ struck up then, and the congregation rumbled to its feet. Joe reappeared at the end of the pew, but Jules insisted on moving out of the way so that he could stand between them. 'Blessed art thou amongst women' Jules said to him and he laughed; Ash had heard the expression used in Italian but it was Joe who had explained that it came from the Hail Mary. Then their heads swivelled as Donatella swept up the aisle on her father's arm, in lace-covered silk. The train was part of the dress, and so long that it made the bride look taller. The back was cut in a deep vee, exposing a lot of Donatella's caramel skin and smooth muscle. She and Gianni took their places on those strange seats, which Ash now realised were kneelers. Both bowed their heads before the priest. Jules leaned across Joe and said in an exaggerated whisper, 'He looks as if he's waiting to get his head chopped off.'

'Ssh!' said Ash, hoping the people in front weren't very good at English, or if they were, that they were too polite to let on that they understood. Joe though was smiling.

A fussing middle-aged woman in a suit a little too tight for her, slipped out of her pew a couple of rows in front of them and arranged the train across the lozenged marble. A camera flashed, and the great pageant of Gianni and Donatella's wedding began.

'I'm amazed that Gianni has all these friends,' whispered Ash to Joe as they proceeded up the magnificent marble staircase of the hotel, part of an unstoppable flow of elegantly dressed and perfumed Venetians. 'I've only ever seen him with Donatella or with Davide. It looks as though the hotel has been taken over just for them.'

'They'll be his friends from school and university. I couldn't muster up the same number of guests. I've moved around too much, lost touch with people. But they'll probably only be together like this for each other's weddings. And eventually, one by one, they'll attend each other's funerals.'

Ash glanced at him. 'That's a grim thought,' she said, thinking of a sombre motor-boat she'd seen gliding across the water to the cemetery island of San Michele. 'This *is* lovely, all of this, but if it was me, I don't think I'd want all of this fuss, never mind the expense. I'd want something more intimate.'

'I would too—'

Ash could see his lips moving but by now they had moved into the great hall of the *piano nobile* where the babble of the staircase had turned into a roar. A waitress was handing them flutes of prosecco and a colleague of hers was asking them for their names for the seating plan. Ashley and Joe found themselves on a circular table with Juliet and Davide and two couples who were friends of Gianni's from school but who had spent time in Dublin and London to work in banking and for one of the big teaching hospitals, though Lidia, the surgeon, had returned home. Ash learned that best man speeches weren't required in Italy, though Davide went back and forth to the top table in the breaks between courses. The clatter of voices subsided to a convivial hum, as guests tucked into delicious food that Ash recognised – dishes from the restaurant across the square.

'How could you ever leave Venice?' Ash asked Lidia.

'I did it for the joy of coming back again. And to learn, of course. Your NHS is something to be proud of, though it's sorely in need of help now. Here we get the basics right, I think. Our hospitals are clean. We're good at preventive medicine, screening and so forth. But to understand the latest research and to have something to bring back, you have to travel. If it hadn't been London it would have been America, but we decided we didn't want to be more than a two and something hour flight from home.' Lidia took a sip of her wine. 'I shouldn't be talking shop though. I've been longing to ask you – where did you get that fabulous dress?'

When finally the guests spilled out into the square into the velvety warm evening, looking in all their finery like a flock of tropical birds, Juliet took Ash's arm and said, 'Davide is offering us a nightcap. And I had a hundred business cards in my clutch. I've given them all out!'

They sat down at the table where it had all begun. Then Ash looked up, not thinking about the webcam but nevertheless sure they were being watched. At an open window in the building opposite, a sad little shaggy face looked out.

'Oh no, there's poor Killer!'

'Don't worry,' smiled Davide. 'I've been in to feed him already. He's just annoyed he's not getting to join in the fun.'

Chapter Twenty-eight

Ponte di Rialto

Three days later

'Look over there, Joe. On that post.'

Joe followed Ashley's pointing finger. It was dusk, a beautiful velvety grey blue evening. They were standing on the outside steps of the Rialto Bridge. Behind them they could hear the murmur of voices and the footfall of the people on the central part, where the shops were still open.

'The seagull?'

'Yes. I used to watch him during lockdown. The webcam must be just behind him.'

'How do you know it's the same one?'

'I don't. I just like to think that he is. Perhaps any old seagull gets to perch on there. Perhaps he's the fifty-ninth one I've seen there.'

'If I'd found that post I think I'd stick to it.' Joe's arm stole around Ash's waist, and she leaned into him. Joe, so big, solid, dependable – and, as he'd demonstrated again last night, a graceful, considerate and sensitive lover.

She looked up at him and his face came down to meet hers.

'When will you be back?' he murmured eventually.

'Oh. Christmas? But you'll be over next month. It depends a bit on those premises downstairs.'

'Things take a while here but that should be sorted early in the new year.'

'If that comes off, I'll be as bad as Gianni.'

'How so?'

'Worse. He comes out of his front door and crosses the campo to go to work. I'll come downstairs, turn right and unlock the next shopfront.'

'As long as you don't get bored of it,' said Joe quietly.

'I won't.'

'Or of me.'

Ash put her hand to his cheek. 'No. Because you're the least boring person I know.'

'I'm afraid of rushing things with you, though. It's having had to wait so long.'

'I never asked you – so much happened that night – but when you introduced me to Wanda as your *fidanzata*, what did you mean?'

Joe paused. 'Nothing and everything, really. Whatever you'd want it to mean. I don't want to do an Ed, you see, and make assumptions.'

'I do love you, Joe. I should tell you more often. It's just that Ed used to make me say it, you see. It's as if he was looking for validation the whole time.'

'And here's me just about asking the same thing.'

'It doesn't feel like that with you. But remember I told you how Ed had everything worked out? Even to the two point two kids, poor little things, and me not going back to work? I was this bit of his jigsaw puzzle to be slotted in. I don't think I really existed beyond the picture on the top of the box, if you get me. I'd want to be with you on an equal footing. Does that make sense?'

'Perfect sense, my serious, gorgeous Ashley.'

She looked at him wondering if she'd detected a trace of mockery, but he was just Joe, saying gravely exactly what he thought. A vaporetto chugged out from under the bridge at that moment. She gazed down at the roof, and at the people in the stern, remembering how she and the seagull had watched those boats go back and forth almost empty, in those dark, empty months.

'There's the ninety day rule anyway,' she said. 'I suppose it means in theory I could spend half the year here if you add it all up. Ninety days out of a hundred and eighty.'

'A European husband would mean you could stay here as long as you wanted,' said Joe - a little hoarsely, Ash thought.

'True,' she said, not looking at him.

'They do civil marriages close to here, actually,' he went on. 'You can see the place from the other side of the bridge. The Palazzo Cavalli.'

'Sounds like you've sussed the place out, Joe,' she said, aiming for a jokey tone that came out too nervously. Ash wanted to tread on her own toes as soon as she'd said it.

'I've been to a wedding there, that's all. Photos on a balcony overlooking the Grand Canal. Seventeenth-century plasterwork in the reception rooms. James Fenimore Cooper used to live there.'

'What, the man who wrote *The Last of the Mohicans*?'

'The very same. I suppose I shouldn't be surprised you'd heard of him.'

'I was a bit bookish when I was at school. Spent my lunch hours in the library instead of in the playground. I can't quite imagine Hawkeye in a gondola though.'

'Nor stealing one. It's a bit different from steering a canoe, right enough. He'd have had to stand up. But I don't think that book was written here.'

There was a short silence. In the gathering gloom, Ash thought she saw the seagull scratch under a wing with his beak. She wished she could think of something to ask about that wedding venue.

'About Palazzo Cavalli,' he said, his hand moving up and down on her waist.

'Mmm?'

'It doesn't need to be the mayor that marries you here.

Any Italian citizen can do it. I think they just need to be resident in Venice. A friend, for instance.'

'That's nice,' said Ash. *Lame!*

'This isn't going at all the way I meant it to, Ash. I'm sorry.'

'Joe?'

'I can't even see your face clearly by now to know how much of an arse I'm making of myself.'

'Joe – what do you mean? Then she looked at his stricken face and the penny dropped. 'You aren't proposing by any chance?'

'That was the plan. I nearly did it last night but was afraid you might think I was just talking in what you might call the heat of the moment.'

Ashley snuggled against him. There was safety – well, something more than safety, she thought. More like support, solidarity. Just being there, for her.

'I liked that moment, Joe.'

His arm pulled her closer.

'You did?' She heard the smile in his voice.

'I was hoping we'd have more like it.'

'Tonight?'

'Yes. And yes, Joe.'

'"And yes, Joe" what?'

'Just yes. Now show me this Palazzo Cavalli.'

'It doesn't have to be there, if you wanted somewhere else. Somewhere at home.'

'No, I found you here. At home I'd been too dense to even see you.'

They walked round to the other side of the bridge, and Joe pointed out a palace where three or four gondolas bobbed in the gentle ebb and flow of the water.

'That's it, with the blue and white mooring posts outside.' Lights had been lit inside, but it wasn't the hard, solid glare of office striplights but the gentle, diffused glow of Murano glass chandeliers.

'I was wondering,' said Joe, his voice cracking slightly. 'Perhaps you and Jules could arrive by boat. I'd be waiting for you on the landing stage.'

'Did you want a big bash, Joe?' Ashley could barely believe she was having a conversation like this one. She didn't want that evening to end – well, she did, only because it would end in Joe's bed.

He hesitated. 'I'd do what you wanted, Ash. To be honest, no. Or at least not this one. Just the core people – and our Venice friends.'

Ash quivered with pleasure at that. *Our Venice friends. It's like I'm living here already.*

'And then perhaps a party – or parties – later. London friends and that big streeling mob in Ireland. They'll not be denied, knowing them.'

'Of course. Where would we eat afterwards?' Somehow talking about a 'reception' felt too suburban for the magical place where they were standing.

'Wherever you'd want.'

'In Campo Santa Maria Formosa. Where we met – really met, I mean.'

'Any thoughts about who might perform the ceremony?'

Ashley paused. 'Oh… do they let dogs in?'

'I don't know. We could ask. Killer, you mean? He's pretty well-behaved. So it's Gianni you want? That's a really kind thought, Ash. Donatella will like the importance that gives him too.'

'Or what about Professor Girotti?'

'That's an even better idea. What – what is it, Ash?'

'The reason I mentioned Gianni. You see, he doesn't know this but he's sort of the reason all this happened.'

'*Gianni?*'

'Yes. It's a bit of a story. It all started in lockdown, you see.'

'Let's walk over to Campo Santa Maria Formosa now. The route we'll go on our big day. That's unless you want to go by boat.'

Ash pictured herself in a vintage wedding dress, probably fifties style, adjusted by Juliet to be a perfect fit, walking on Joe's arm. She saw the scene, months from now. He'd be in a dark suit, but somehow he, and it, would be more dashing than the ones he'd worn to Gulliver and Brant, in what felt now like a lifetime away. The crowds along the Salizzada San Lio would part and smile, the shopkeepers come to their doors. The Venetians would applaud and the tourists lift their phones as they passed by, as if they were walking a very long church aisle.

'I'd love the walk.'

'Shall we go? And you can tell me about Gianni on the way.'

Only minutes later, Joe's delighted laughter was echoing off the high walls of the narrow Calle dei Stagneri. That was when Ash noticed that their footsteps on the worn flagstones of the alley had synchronised. It was going to be all right. Everything was going to be all right.

About Kate Zarrelli

Katherine Mezzacappa writing for Romaunce Books under the name Kate Zarrelli is an Irish author currently living in Carrara, northern Tuscany. She holds a BA in History of Art from UEA, an MLitt in English Literature from Durham and a Masters in Creative Writing from Canterbury Christ Church University. Her debut novel (writing as Katie Hutton), The Gypsy Bride, made the last fifteen in the Historical Novel Society's 2018 new novel competition. Her short fiction has been short - and longlisted in numerous competitions, and she has been awarded residencies at Cill Rialaig Artists village by the Irish Writers Centre in 2019 and at Hald Hovedgaard by the Danish Centre for Writers and Translators in 2022.

Katherine's short fiction in a variety of genres has been published worldwide. She has in addition published academically in the field of 19th-century ephemeral illustrated fiction. Katherine is a committee member of the Irish Writers Union and holds professional membership of the Society of Authors, the Historical Novel Society and the Romance Novelists' Association, she is a regular reviewer for the HNS quarterly journal and regularly contributes to the RNA in various ways.

Have you read Kate Zarrelli's first novel?

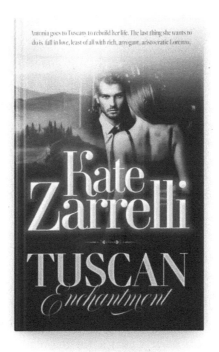

Antonia goes to Tuscany to rebuild her life. The last thing she wants to do is fall in love, least of all with rich, arrogant, aristocratic Lorenzo.

Librarian Antonia Gray has fled England for Tuscany, desperate to put distance between herself, the dangerous man she nearly found herself married to, and the whispers that followed her since his exposure.

She's perfectly happy losing herself in the archive of a seventeenth-century Italian explorer until she meets his descendant, Lorenzo Quattromani. Lorenzo is rich, arrogant, and inconveniently handsome. Worse, he seems determined to make Antonia fall in love with him. The last thing Antonia wants is another man in her life – at least not one living in this century.

But with Lorenzo living under the same roof, he takes every opportunity to prove to Antonia that he isn't the feckless dilettante she first took him for. Antonia struggles resolutely to keep hold of her scornful first impression, but Lorenzo at his most charming proves impossible to resist.

★★★★★
Amazon review
An escapist romance to sweep you off your feet

A classic, escapist romance with beautiful descriptions and a heroine that you want to succeed. Full of well-observed details, vivid characters and realistic drama that keeps the pages turning. a perfect escape for the reader especially in the middle of a dreary British winter.

Have you read Kate Zarrelli's second novel?

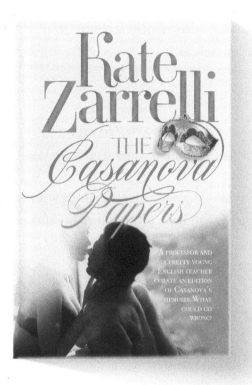

Ellie Murphy gets a job teaching English at a school in Venice where she meets Professor Piero Contarini, suave, sexy, enigmatic and the descendent of an old Venetian family.

She agrees to help him with a project curating a new edition of the memoirs of the famous seducer and ne'er-do-well, Giacomo Casanova.

But taking their task to heart and uncovering some of their own secret fantasies, they start to enact the seducers adventures, with each other, ecstatically revealing their own kinks as they do so.

But who is that watching them from the shadowy alleyways of Venice?

★★★★★

Amazon review
An entertaining and steamy romance

Kate Zarrelli's The Casanova Papers is a scorching page-turner spiced with heat, heart and emotion that will whisk you to Venice and to a world of danger and desire.

Join us at
Romaunce Books

For competitions, interviews and latest updates about our authors and their latest books plus much, much more

Follow us on

https://twitter.com/Romaunce

https://www.instagram.com/romauncebooks

https://www.facebook.com/romaunce

And go to our website to subscribe to our newsletter www.romaunce.com

Let's Talk

Romaunce Books

BV - #0154 - 170924 - C0 - 203/127/17 - PB - 9600198000281 - Matt Lamination